C0A0291761

Murder
Your Darlings

Debbie Young

Copyright Information

MURDER YOUR DARLINGS
by Debbie Young

© Debbie Young 2020
Published by Hawkesbury Press 2020
Hawkesbury Upton, Gloucestershire, England
Cover design by Rachel Lawston of Lawston Design

All rights reserved. No part of this ebook may be
reproduced, stored in a retrieval system, or transmitted in
any form or by any means, electronic, mechanical,
photocopying, recording or otherwise, without the prior
written permission of the author.

This is a work of fiction. Any similarity between the
characters and situations within its pages and places or
persons, living or dead, is unintentional and coincidental.

ISBN 978-1-911223-55-9
Also available as an ebook

About the Author

Debbie Young writes warm, witty, feel-good fiction, inspired by her daily life in the beautiful English Cotswolds.

Her Sophie Sayers Village Mystery series follows the life of the fictitious village of Wendlebury Barrow from one summer to the next, and her Staffroom at St Bride's series will run the course of a school year. She also writes short novellas in the same setting under the series title Tales from Wendlebury Barrow.

Her humorous short stories are available in themed collections, such as *Marry in Haste, Quick Change* and *Stocking Fillers*, and in many anthologies.

She is a frequent speaker at literature festivals and writers' events and is founder and director of the free Hawkesbury Upton Literature Festival.

A regular contributor to two local community magazines, the award-winning *Tetbury Advertiser* and the *Hawkesbury Parish News*, she has published two collections of her columns, *Young by Name* and *All Part of the Charm*. These publications offer insight into her own life in a small Cotswold village where she lives with her Scottish husband and their teenage daughter.

For the latest information about Debbie's
books and events, visit her Writing Life website,
where you may also like to join her free Readers' Club:
www.authordebbieyoung.com

Also by Debbie Young

Sophie Sayers Village Mysteries
Best Murder in Show (1)
Trick or Murder? (2)
Murder in the Manger (3)
Murder by the Book (4)
Springtime for Murder (5)
Murder Lost and Found (7) – coming 2020

Staffroom at St Bride's Series
Secrets at St Bride's (1)
Stranger at St Bride's (2) – coming 2020

Short Story Collections
Marry in Haste
Quick Change
Stocking Fillers

Essay Collections
All Part of the Charm:
        A Modern Memoir of English Village Life
Young By Name:
        Whimsical Columns from the Tetbury Advertiser

To Jessica Bell,
author, poet, musician and muse,
and in fond memory of my Greek school friend,
Vasilios Chakos, who sadly passed away
before I could tell him that
I'd borrowed his name in this book

"Whenever you feel an impulse to perpetrate
a piece of exceptionally fine writing,
obey it—whole-heartedly—
and delete it before sending
your manuscript to press.
Murder your darlings."
Sir Arthur Quiller-Couch

"Always look a Trojan horse in the mouth."
Sophie Sayers

Nothing is sweeter than home.
Homer

Murder
Your
Darlings

1 A Greek Cliffhanger

"Sophie, you didn't!"

"What?"

"Push Marina off the cliff."

Ben's voice behind me made me jump. Too engrossed in listening to my voicemail messages, I hadn't heard him coming up the hillside track.

He pointed at the solitary flip-flop, balanced on the edge of the cliff. It was as turquoise as the Ionian Sea surrounding this tiny Greek island. Beside it lay Marina Milanese's smartphone in its distinctive diamanté case, a jagged crack dividing the screen diagonally.

Ben took a step closer to me.

"Was it because you were jealous of her success as a bestselling novelist? What a great story that would be!"

"Don't be ridiculous, Ben. Just because I'm standing near her shoe and her phone doesn't mean I pushed her off the cliff. Why do you journalists have to make such a drama out of everything?"

Ben strode past the old windmill to peer down at the sea.

"Well, she's definitely gone over. Look, there's her other flip-flop, caught on a ledge halfway down."

I'd have to take his word for it, not daring to go as close as he did to the sheer drop. This was the highest point on Floros.

"What about the rest of her?"

Turning to face me, he shrugged. "No sign of her body, but then I wouldn't expect there to be. There's no beach below us. The sea comes right up to the cliffs. If she wasn't unconscious before she hit the water, the rocks beneath the surface will have knocked her out. Lured by the sirens to a watery grave – what a fitting end for a leading romantic novelist!"

He passed his hands across his eyes as he turned his back to the sea.

"I think you're being over-dramatic, Ben. Marina told me she was a strong swimmer. Surely if she fell into the sea, she'd just swim around the headland to the harbour? It can't be far."

"Not a chance. No-one could survive a fall like that, not even an Olympic swimmer."

We were silent for a moment.

"Do you think her body will reappear down there at low tide?"

He shot me a reproving look.

"The Ionian Sea isn't tidal."

"Oh no, of course not. I forgot."

As I knelt down to examine Marina's phone, Ben held up his hands in warning.

"Sophie, don't touch it! You'll leave fingerprints. Talk about incriminating yourself!"

"Sorry." My voice was small in the warm breeze. I took the light cotton sarong that I'd found on a hedge on the way up and wrapped it around the phone, careful not to disturb the compromised screen.

Ben pointed to scuff marks in the dusty soil around where Marina's phone had landed.

"Look, there are signs of a struggle." He pulled his own phone out of his pocket to photograph the evidence. Before he could click on his camera app, a pair of goats, neck-bells jangling, trotted out from among a clump of pine trees and straight across the patch of disturbed soil, erasing any evidence. I leapt to my feet to get out of their way.

"Those marks are probably just goats' footprints. These goats get everywhere."

Their demonic rectangular pupils spooked me. "Perhaps the goats pushed Marina off the cliff?"

When Ben took a step towards them, they turned coy and skittered back in amongst the trees.

Ben rubbed his stubbly chin for a moment.

"I don't suppose you heard anything on your way up here? No sounds of camera shutter clicking or of her talking to anyone on the phone? If so, that would suggest she plummeted to her death just before you reached the summit."

I shuddered. There was no need to converse in the lurid language of tabloid newspapers.

"No, nothing. That's why I was heading up here – for a bit of solitude. The only sounds I could hear weren't human: the creaking of the old windmill, the rustling of the undergrowth, and the tinkling of goat bells."

"Are you sure you weren't trying to get Marina alone? As this is the only place on the island where you can get a mobile signal, we all knew she would head here at our first break."

I folded my arms across my chest. The last thing I wanted was more one-to-one time with Marina, after the embarrassing incident on the plane.

"For goodness' sake, Ben, why do you have to sensationalise everything? I know for a fact she was short-sighted but wouldn't wear glasses. You know what Marina was like with selfies for her social media accounts. She might have been so busy posing that she took a step too far back. Chances are it was a tragic accident."

I flinched as I realised I was speaking about Marina in the past tense already.

"Of course, there have been press reports of accidents like that every holiday season since the invention of the selfie. But accident or murder, one thing's for sure: the disappearance of Marina Milanese will be international headline news – and as the only member of the press on the island, I plan to land the scoop."

2 Sophie's Odyssey

The previous week

Once I'd got over the initial excitement of winning my free place in the competition, I hadn't really wanted to come on this writers' retreat.

"Are you sure it's not transferable?"

I leaned on the trade counter, fixing Hector with as appealing a gaze as I could muster. I knew he had a thing about my eyes. But now he avoided them, swivelling around on his stool to flick through the order book on the shelf behind him.

"Absolutely not, sweetheart. You won the place fair and square, and I'm not about to take that from you."

"But you're the real writer here, not me. I shall feel a fraud pitching up at a writers' retreat. The others will soon rumble that I'm not in their league."

Hector closed the order book and returned it to the shelf.

"How do you know what they'll be like? They might be even less experienced than you."

I could have done without the 'even'. Sensing my irritation, he sought to stop digging his inadvertent hole.

"What I mean is, you won your place on merit. The writing magazine wouldn't have given you the prize if they didn't think you were up to it."

"Merit? The only evidence they had of my supposed writing talent wasn't even a complete sentence: *Eat My Words: the Confessions of an Encyclopaedia Salesman*. A

5

throwaway line, a joke, and not a very good one. You bamboozled me."

Hector couldn't argue with that. He'd simply borrowed my quip without my permission and entered it into the writing magazine's competition to dream up a fun book title. The first I had known about it was when he told me I'd won a free place on a spring writing retreat on Ithaca.

He tried a conciliatory smile.

"Maybe they just want you as a foil to make the others look better."

That didn't help.

To be fair, I had no doubt that Hector's intentions had been honourable. He knew I wanted to write books, just like my Great Auntie May, the famous travel writer whose cottage I'd inherited the previous summer. May had helped Hector set up Hector's House, his bookshop in the village, providing start-up capital and moral support. He'd tried to repay her kindness by giving me a job in his bookshop and by encouraging me to pursue my writing ambitions. Falling in love with me was an unintended consequence.

I was nowhere near as confident as he was in my potential as a writer, having only just started to take my writing seriously. I'd joined the village writers' group to spur me on, but most of its members were no further forward than I was. Since my move to Wendlebury Barrow, the only work I'd shared in public was a nativity play that had resulted in the whole village being accused of murder and *Travels with My Aunt's Garden*, my monthly seasonal nature-notes column in the parish magazine, inspired by my aunt's cottage garden. I didn't count the half-finished novels I'd brought with me to my new home, nor the stash of short stories piling up on my aunt's old writing desk. I'd never shown them to anyone else, not even Hector. *Especially* not Hector.

In the meantime, Hector, writing under his secret pseudonym, had completed and published two more romantic novels and continued to be a bestselling fiction author, at least in his own bookshop. The most recent he'd dedicated to me, *The Girl with Forget-Me-Not Eyes*. He was far more deserving of a place on the retreat than I was. But he'd told everyone I was going, to make sure I didn't back out.

***

"A writers' retreat? What's that?"

Jemima is one of the village children who come to me in the bookshop after school for extra reading lessons.

"Is it like hide-and-seek for people who write books?"

I laughed.

"I suppose there is an element of hiding. All the writers go away on holiday together so that they can get on with their writing in peace."

Jemima considered for a moment.

"So what will you write when you get there? Will it be a children's book? I'd like it best if it was, so I could read it."

For a moment she had me stumped. I'd been so busy fretting about going on the retreat at all that I hadn't thought about the practicalities. The organisers of the retreat, the Stacey Sydney Agency, hadn't briefed us about that side of things. They'd just provided a timetable of the daily talks to be given by Stacey herself, and a guest bestselling writer whose name was yet to be revealed. The talks were to take a couple of hours each morning. The rest of the week, we would be free to write.

I forced a smile.

"I expect inspiration will strike me while I'm there."

Jemima nodded. At least she believed in me, or so I thought, until she reached into her pencil case and drew out a large pink eraser in the shape of a unicorn's head, its horn slightly blunted from use.

"Here, this is a going-away present for you. In case you make any mistakes while you're there."

By the time I returned, the unicorn would be a horse.

***

"You are lucky, Sophie."

Karen topped up my cup of tea at the Wendlebury Writers' meeting, held in the bookshop's tearoom. For a moment I almost offered her my place on the retreat. She was one of the few published members of our group, a regular contributor of short stories to women's magazines.

"You must keep a journal while you're there so you can tell us all about it when you come back."

She gave a slight nod to the group's leader, Dinah, who on this cue produced from her messenger bag a beautiful hardback travel diary, its cover design inspired by vintage luggage labels.

"Following in your aunt's footsteps, eh?" Dinah gave a rare smile as she set the diary down on the table in front of me. "I think May Sayers would be very pleased for you."

"And proud," added Bella.

I grimaced. "I haven't actually done anything yet."

My parting gift from Billy, a regular customer of the bookshop's tearoom, was more pragmatic. As I served up his morning coffee the next day, he slipped a small cardboard box into my hand.

"In the past, I've found a pack of these very helpful on my holidays."

Hector, seated at the trade counter, looked up from his laptop. His startled expression relaxed when he saw the brand name on the box.

"I hope Sophie won't be needing too many sachets of hangover remedy, Billy. Stay off the ouzo, sweetheart, and keep your head clear for what you're there for. It's a writers' retreat, not a Club 18–30 holiday."

Billy stirred more cream into his coffee.

"Don't listen to him, girlie. He just wants you to behave yourself while he's not there. Do you good to get out from under his shadow for a change."

"I'm not under his shadow," I protested.

But Billy was right. Hector and I worked together every day the shop was open and spent most evenings and many nights together. The only time we'd been separated for more than twenty-four hours was when I'd celebrated Christmas at my parents' house in Inverness. Had my relationship with Hector become too easy, too comfortable? Had I fallen into this cosy life with him too quickly? Was it really something I wanted to last long-term? A little time apart might do us good.

The retreat would give me fresh perspective on our future together. While Hector seemed to have no ambitions beyond keeping his shop afloat until he retired, its fluctuating profits shored up by the royalties from his novels, I had yet to feel as settled. Before I'd moved to Wendlebury, I was constantly on the move, relocating to a different European city each academic year to teach English as a foreign language in international schools. After nearly a year in the village, I was beginning to realise that I was ready to don my backpack and venture off to foreign parts again. Greece was somewhere I'd always wanted to visit. And the trip was free, too. How could I be so ungrateful? I really shouldn't look a gift horse in the mouth. Unless of course it's a Trojan horse. One should always look a Trojan horse in the mouth.

In her career as a travel writer, my aunt was forever on the move. She used her cottage in Wendlebury only as a pit stop between assignments and research trips, breaking the heart of the local lad who hankered after her return (now my elderly neighbour, Joshua). Would that prove to be my destiny – and Hector's – too? Would Auntie May's genes come out in me yet, and not just as a writer?

I was about to find out.

3 Leaving on a Jet Plane

"Don't worry, I'll look after him while you're gone."

Hector's godmother, Kate, had volunteered to man the shop on the morning of my departure so that Hector could drive me to Bristol Airport.

"Just relax and enjoy yourself. You deserve a proper holiday. You never take time off from this wretched shop. Hector must owe you weeks of leave."

Kate was right. Although theoretically I was entitled to a day off each week in return for working on Saturday, I seldom took it, preferring to spend the time with Hector. Or was it more out of boredom, given that I would otherwise be stuck in the village with little public transport and no car, or indeed driving licence, to take me anywhere else?

"And don't let him put you to work the minute you come back. Take a day or two to rest up and regroup. Don't let your holiday end any sooner than it has to."

Hector sighed as he handed her the shop keys. "What about me? Don't I deserve some time off?"

As she went behind the trade counter to take up Hector's usual post, Kate rolled her eyes. "OK, take the rest of the morning off. Off you go, the pair of you – and here, Sophie, here's a little something to give you a head start on the other writers."

She pulled out of her soft leather handbag a slender parcel wrapped in mauve tissue paper and tied with silver thread.

Hector jangled his car keys impatiently. "You'd better open it now, rather than attempt to go through airport security with an unopened parcel wrapped by a stranger."

Kate laughed. "I'm not really trying to land you in a Greek prison, Sophie."

She sat down on a stool behind the trade counter, resting her chin on her hands to watch me untie the gift. I slipped off the thread and opened up the paper to reveal an old-fashioned cardboard box with the familiar Parker pen brand embossed on the lid. Inside lay a black lacquered propelling pencil with gold trim, resting on a scarlet satin cushion.

"There are spare leads beneath the cushion," Kate explained.

I set the box down on the counter and carefully lifted the pencil from its little bed. As I turned it over in my hands, my eyes filled with tears.

"It was Auntie May's." My lower lip trembled. "It's got May Sayers engraved on it."

Kate smiled, gratified.

"May gave it to me a long time ago. I thought it belonged with you now. Besides, I never write in pencil."

"Far too sure of yourself," murmured Hector.

Kate ignored him.

"May swore by perpetual pencil for writing on the move."

"She always wrote to me from home in fountain pen," I remembered.

"Bottles of ink and travelling bags are not a good mix, unless you only ever wear royal blue," said Kate. "Now, off you go, write loads, and have fun." She came out from behind the counter to give me a hug. "And above all, come home safe. God knows, the bookshop won't cope without you for long."

When she winked at me, I realised 'bookshop' was her code for Hector. I wasn't sure that I felt equal to that responsibility.

I'd already stowed my backpack and cabin bag in Hector's Land Rover, ready for a quick getaway.

"Who's feeding Blossom while you're away?" he asked as we pulled out from his short drive beside the shop on to the High Street. "Not me, I hope."

Hector was more of a dog person, only tolerating Blossom, the black rescue kitten that Billy had bestowed on me back at Easter.

"Joshua. I thought he'd be glad of the company. He doesn't get out much these days. But feel free to look in on her if you miss her."

I bit back a smile, knowing Hector would welcome a cat-free week, although Blossom's presence hadn't prevented him spending the previous night at mine for an extended farewell. Blossom might be glad of a week with no rival for space on my bed too.

"Tommy did offer to mind her, but I said I'd already asked Joshua." Tommy was the local teenage tearaway with a good heart but dubious methods and no sense of danger.

"Good choice," said Hector.

We drove on in silence for a bit. I gazed affectionately at the Cotswold stone houses, glowing in the spring sunshine, before we joined the M5, heading south to the functional urban sprawl of Bristol. I felt slightly awkward, wondering whether we should be having an earnest conversation about our mutual commitment before I took off for a week.

"I'll send you a postcard," was the best I could come up with, as he negotiated the winding one-way system that took us across the city to the airport road. When I spotted an aeroplane ascending in the distance, my stomach flipped. Soon I'd be up in the sky too, heading off for a new adventure and who knew what outcome? I laid a hand on Hector's thigh, solidly reassuring within his jeans.

Anxious to get back to his beloved shop, Hector wanted to stop for the bare minimum of time to drop me off. After we'd pulled into the short-stay car park, he lifted my backpack from the boot and hoisted it onto my shoulders, then handed me my cabin bag.

"You don't mind if I don't come into Departures with you, do you?"

I shook my head as if I really didn't mind.

"I'm a big girl now, Hector."

Then he stepped forward to wrap his arms round me and my backpack in a close, tight hug, pressing me full-length against him. I wished his hands were on the bare flesh of my back rather than on my lumpy backpack, and I shivered with pleasure as I remembered our prolonged embraces of the night before. Suddenly a week apart felt a very long time.

A car horn beeped to interrupt our kiss. I hadn't realised we were holding up the traffic, drivers keen to escape the barrier before their allotted time ran out. Hector waved thanks to the tooting driver and steered me to the pavement, one arm looped across my shoulders, resting on top of the backpack.

"I guess I'd better let you go," he said, smiling gently. My heart melted afresh under the scrutiny of his green eyes. "A whole week, eh? I'm really going to miss you."

"I'll miss you too."

"Here's a little something to read on the plane."

From the back pocket of his jeans, he pulled out a tiny midnight-blue vintage hardback with gold lettering on the spine. Homer's *Odyssey*. He pressed it into my hands then gave them a final squeeze.

"*Kalo taksidi*, Sophie."

"Eh?"

"That's Greek for bon voyage."

"How did you know that?"

He grinned. "Travel section. Greek phrasebook, second shelf down. I slipped one of those in your cabin bag too, by the way. Bon voyage, and make the most of the opportunity."

All too soon he was climbing back into his Land Rover. I raised my hand in farewell and watched him rev up, pull out and drive away till his Land Rover disappeared from view. Looking down at the book in my hands, I flipped it open, and read his inscription.

"*To the girl with forget-me-not eyes. Come home safe and come home soon. Love always, Homer.*"

There can't be many people in possession of a signed copy of Homer's *Odyssey*. Hector had dressed up as Homer for the fancy-dress carnival in last year's village show. To me, the little volume couldn't have been more precious if it had been signed by the ancient Greek himself.

I hitched my backpack a little further up my back and stepped out into the busy flow of passengers heading for Departures.

4 Take Off

Once past check-in and security, I found myself gravitating towards the airport's bookshop, as if seeking a home from home.

But the airport bookshop was nothing like Hector's House. Glaringly bright lights, instead of soft creamy bulbs; cold metal shelves, instead of old oak; the only soundtrack the pinging of alerts over the tannoy calling flights, instead of Hector's gentle background music, each track chosen to match a visiting customer's tastes. And of course, there was no bookshop tearoom for shoppers to stop in and gossip. I knew which shop I'd rather see my books stocked in – if I ever wrote any.

For a few moments, I stood back and watched travellers come and go, grabbing chunky paperbacks with barely a glance at the contents. The books were flying off the shelves, appropriately enough.

I surveyed the titles. All were big name blockbusters, none of them bestsellers in Hector's House. Hector told me that publishers pay big bucks and offer steep discounts to secure spots in airport bookshops. The sales justified the investment.

I couldn't stop myself from falling into work mode and tidying up the display, aligning spines and reshelving those that careless browsers had put back in the wrong place. Someone had mistakenly shoved into the number one spot a copy of *Doctor of Love*, the latest offering from Marina Milanese, whose name always made me picture an Italian fish dish. I knew her books were popular, but they weren't *that* popular. I put it back where it should have been, in the unnumbered shelves opposite.

My own inflight reading already catered for, I left the bookshop, found a comfy seat and settled down with Homer's *Odyssey* until my flight was called. I wondered whether the original Homer had looked as good in a toga as Hector did in his fancy dress at the village show. Would they have village shows on Ithaca? I read the first page about ten times without really taking it in.

The departure lounge was not the easiest place in which to get lost in a book. I set *The Odyssey* down on my lap and gazed about me. People watching is good practice for novelists, so this counted as research. There would be plenty of time in the coming week to catch up with Homer.

As people pottered about the shops and cafés, I played my usual airport game of matching travellers to the destinations listed on the departures board. Its screen constantly refreshed as flights departed, every take-off moving my flight to Kefalonia – the closest airport to Ithaca – one tantalizing notch up the board. The crowd downing alcopops and pints of beer could go to Ibiza. I'd despatch families with excited young children to Paris for Disneyland. Elegant slender women might appreciate a trip to Milan. I didn't care to send anyone to the less glamorous destinations on the board. If it was left to me, those flights would be empty.

As a plane took off to Glasgow and all the others moved up a line on the board, a flight to Inverness appeared at the bottom of the screen. Suddenly I missed my parents, who worked at the university there. I hadn't seen them since New Year's Day. I made a mental note to rectify that on my return. It would be good to be back in Inverness, filling my lungs with the clear, fresh air from the River Ness as it rushed past my parents' house towards the Beauly Firth. Was Scotland my second home now, displaced by Wendlebury Barrow in less than a year? I wondered what Hector might make of Scotland – if I could persuade him to leave his precious shop for long enough to visit.

Breaking my reverie, a huddle of Irishmen in rugby tops, no doubt Dublin-bound, began to celebrate the previous night's victory with a song, only to be interrupted by the tannoy.

"Would all passengers for flight BJ721 to Kefalonia now proceed to Gate 3, where your flight is ready for boarding."

Shouldering my cabin bag, I marched swiftly to the gate. As I arrived, I scanned the queue for fellow writers. Perhaps I was the only delegate to be flying from Bristol. I couldn't see anyone else who looked likely. What did a writer look like, anyway? Did I look like one?

Plenty of my fellow passengers appeared to be readers. One middle-aged woman seemed gripped by the Marina Milanese novel I'd re-shelved in the airport bookshop. Another was deep in a book about geology. To each his own.

The queue was completely stationary, so to put the wait to constructive use, I slipped *The Odyssey* into my jacket pocket and extracted my Greek phrasebook from my cabin bag. On my travels around Europe as an English language teacher, I'd liked to learn a little of my host country's language, partly out of courtesy but mostly to make life easier for myself. I already knew how to ask directions to the ladies' toilets in French, German, Spanish, Portuguese, and Dutch. Now I should add Greek to my repertoire.

Opening the phrasebook at the first page, I recognised an addition in Hector's distinctive handwriting:

"*έχω φίλο (pronounced echo filo) = I have a boyfriend.*"

I smiled. I did indeed, and I was missing him already.

I was just about to pull out my phone and text Hector to thank him for the lift and the books, when two ground crew emerged from a staff-only door to take up their duties at the boarding desks. The queue began to shuffle forward before they'd even let anyone through.

Slower to advance than the couple in front of me, I found myself queue-jumped by the Marina Milanese fan, who until now had remained seated. Flashing an insincere smile, she manoeuvred her designer-label vanity case just in front of me, treading on my toes in the process. When I squealed in pain, she was unapologetic.

"Oh, for heaven's sake, it doesn't matter where we are in the queue. We've all got allocated seats, so I'm not putting you at a disadvantage by going in front of you."

My toes begged to differ, but not wanting to make a scene, I made an effort to be conciliatory.

"Airport reading, eh?" I nodded at the book in her hands. "What is that bookshop manager thinking? Always the same formulaic stuff, wherever you fly from."

"Oh, I don't know. I think this is one of her best."

She tapped the author's name, spelled out in a curvy, flirtatious font on the front cover.

"*Doctor of Love.*" She enunciated the title as if I might need help reading it.

The cover illustration distracted me from the title.

"That seems a bit unlikely, don't you think? They'd never let a nurse in an operating theatre with such thick make-up and those dangly earrings. And she's wearing false eyelashes. Supposing one fell into a patient during an operation?"

The woman's tone was cold.

"Are you a medic?"

"No."

"Well, then."

I tried again.

"To be honest I've never read any of her books." I smiled sweetly. "I tend to read whatever my local bookseller recommends. He's never mentioned this author before."

Hector had been pressing books upon me ever since he'd offered me my job. Some might find his attitude patronising, but I liked it. His recommendations were always spot on and, as for this trip, timely. I'd been so busy deciding which notebooks and pens to bring that I'd forgotten to pack anything to read. I pulled *The Odyssey* out of my pocket and waved it at her.

"Homer." I tried not to sound as smug as I felt.

"Simpson?" She didn't look as if she was joking.

"No –" I began, before realising I didn't know what Homer's surname was. Perhaps Homer *was* his surname.

To my relief, a long-winded announcement over the tannoy made further conversation impossible. I returned to my phrasebook, pretending to be engrossed. The queue-jumper held her novel close to her face and continued reading, probably too vain to wear glasses.

At last the queue began to move, and when we reached the desk, she and I parted company, to be processed by different ground crew, me on the right and her on the left.

I held out my passport and boarding card. "*Kalimera*," That's Greek for 'good morning'.

"Mornin', love," returned the attendant in broad Yorkshire, but his smile was appreciative all the same. He sent me to board ahead of the queue-jumper, who was held up as her attendant took a call on his walkie-talkie.

Glad to have a window seat, I buckled up and sat back ready to enjoy the take-off and whatever views the weather permitted. It was a longish flight, over three hours. There'd be plenty of time to make headway with *The Odyssey en route*.

A kerfuffle in the crowded gangway made me look up from my book to see a large vanity case brandished like a weapon at head height as its owner pushed past all those busy stowing their own bags in the overhead lockers. As the vanity case halted beside my seat, I recognised the body beneath it: the queue-jumper.

The woman threw her book on to the seat beside mine, then reached up to the locker above my head, so far occupied only by my bag. She shoved it roughly aside to give hers pride of place. Then she plunged her expensively dressed bottom into the seat next to me, removing her book only at the last minute.

Apparently not recognising me, she held up the book, front cover towards me, and beamed.

"Perfect in-flight reading," she declared.

In silence, unsmiling, I held up *The Odyssey*.

While the cabin crew marched up and down doing safety checks, we immersed ourselves in our books. It was like being in a staring competition. I wanted her to be first to put her book down, proving my reading matter was better than hers. By the time we'd started taxiing to our runway, I'd got as far as page two: progress indeed.

5 Flight of Fancy

Although I was seated at the centre of the plane, just in front of the left wing, a beaming flight attendant wheeled her cart straight past everyone in front of us and drew to a halt only when she reached our row. She focussed exclusively on my neighbour, who still held her book close to her face.

"Excuse me, Miss Milanese." The flight attendant spoke with deference. "I've only just seen your name on the passenger list. I'm sorry we can't offer you an upgrade, as this flight is entirely economy class, but please accept this small gift with our compliments, to thank you for choosing Bargain Jet."

The attendant flipped down my neighbour's tray table and set upon it a miniature bottle of champagne, a plastic champagne flute and a bag of pistachios. Seeing me watching this transaction, the flight attendant kindly included me in her smile, before producing a second bottle, glass and nuts for me.

"And one for your companion too."

"Thank you," I faltered, a little embarrassed.

"Our pleasure."

The attendant returned her admiring gaze to Marina Milanese and pointed at the book.

"That's your latest, isn't it? I can't wait to read it. Of course, my favourite has to be *Love in the Skies*, but in my job I would say that, wouldn't I?"

She giggled coyly.

"I hope you don't mind, Miss Milanese, but I'd better serve the rest of the passengers now. If you need a refill or if I can help in any way, don't hesitate to press the call button in the overhead panel."

She pointed to the button. Flight attendants probably point at things even in their sleep.

"Thank you, I shall."

Marina set her book face down on her tray table and watched her admirer retreat to the front of the plane. There she fell into excited conversation with a colleague, pointing and smiling at Marina, before resuming her duties. The man across the aisle leaned over to scrutinise the author photo on the back of Marina's book.

"My wife thought it was you, but we didn't like to intrude. I expect you always get recognised and given VIP treatment."

Marina sighed as if fame made her life a trial.

"People are so kind. It would seem churlish to refuse." She lay one hand affectionately on her book, clasping her champagne flute in the other. "Still, I suppose when one writes a book lionising airline staff, one can hardly be surprised if they return the favour in kind." She flashed a long-suffering smile at him. "Not that I court special treatment."

He nodded towards her reading material. "Though it must give the game away if they see you reading your own book?"

She gazed down at it, feigning surprise, as if she hadn't realised it was one of her own. The man looked past her to catch my eye and gave me a knowing wink.

"Always something sensational to read on the plane, eh?" He was speaking as much to me as to her.

Then the man's wife nudged him and whispered in his ear. He leaned across the aisle again.

"My wife's just reading one of yours now and wonders whether you'd be so kind as to sign it?"

Marina was practically purring.

"Of course. What name should I sign it to?"

She gave a little wave to the man's wife as he passed the book across.

"Jayne with a Y, please," said the man, before spelling it out to be on the safe side. "J-A-Y-N-E."

To Janey, wrote Marina in purple ink with a diamanté-encrusted gold fountain pen. *With much love, Marina Milanese*. She blew on the ink to dry it before returning the book, open at the signature, to the man's outstretched hand.

When he saw what she had written, he opened his mouth to protest at her error, but thought better of it.

His wife leaned across him.

"Thank you so much, Miss Milanese. My friends at my book club will be dead jealous."

Marina dismissed her thanks with a regal wave.

"My pleasure, my dear."

Then she turned to face me, her back to the couple, as if to indicate the end of their royal audience. Perhaps talking to me seemed the lesser of the two evils. She raised her champagne flute, now nearly empty, in a toast, before pressing the call button for a free refill for us both.

It was going to be a long journey.

6 Kindred Spirits

As the plane began its descent towards Kefalonia, the stunning view of the Ionian Sea, studded with rocky outcrops and islands, was a welcome distraction from my flight companion. I had never before seen sea so truly aquamarine.

Suddenly my competition win seemed real for the first time and Ithaca a real destination rather than a mythical one. Soon I'd be a step closer to my dream of becoming a real writer. Why had I ever resisted?

As soon as the plane had taxied to a halt at its terminal stand, even before the "fasten seatbelt" signs had been extinguished, there began a frenzy of passengers reclaiming luggage from the overhead lockers. I stayed in my seat until Marina had grabbed her vanity case and shoved her way up the aisle towards the front exit. I watched her pause for the crew to take selfies with her, destined no doubt for Bargain Flight's social media pages, as well as their own. When the pilot emerged from the cockpit to whisk her on to the flight deck, Marina, in a hail of girlish giggles, pulled out her own phone to take a selfie with him for her own use.

My cabin bag in one hand and my jacket in the other, I was almost the last to teeter down the front steps to the tarmac, which was shimmering with heat haze. The temperature hit me like a wall, and I reeled slightly, wishing I'd drunk more water and less champagne on the flight.

"You dropped this," said a young woman behind me, holding out *The Odyssey*. It must have slipped out of my jacket pocket. She glanced at the lavish cover illustration of an ancient Greek ship, its sail embossed in gold with a stylised eye.

"Looks a bit highbrow for poolside reading," she said, falling into step beside me as we approached the tiny terminal building.

I grinned. "I'm not going to be spending much time poolside this week. I've come to work."

"Really?" Her face fell in sympathy. "Are you a tour guide or a waitress or something?"

"Oh no, nothing like that. I'm here for a writing course. A writers' retreat. I'm expecting it to be hard work."

She wrinkled her nose and transferred her soft leather messenger bag from her left side to her right.

"I do hope not. I'm doing one too. I thought it was meant to be restful."

I held the terminal door open for her. It wasn't much cooler inside.

"Perhaps it's the same retreat? At the Hotel Ola Kala?"

She stopped just inside the building and clapped her hands in childlike excitement.

"Yes, that's right. Oh, thank goodness! Now I'll know at least one person on the course."

I smiled. I knew how she felt.

"I'm Sophie, by the way."

"I'm Lydia. Lovely to meet you, Sophie."

A drowsy border control officer waved us through the barrier without looking at our passports, and we crossed the small hall to the baggage carousel. Our flight number was already on the board, our plane the only one on the tarmac. Lydia and I slipped into a gap in the circle of passengers surrounding the conveyor luggage belt.

"What sort of thing do you write, Lydia?" I hoped we had something in common, apart from being of a similar age and build. Her hair was as long as mine, but darker and curly, cascading over her shoulders extravagantly; her wide brown eyes were shining.

She wrinkled her delicate nose.

"To be honest, nothing as yet, though I thought I might have a stab at a play. Actually, it wasn't my idea to come on this course. My husband booked it as a surprise present to introduce me to a new hobby."

That struck me as high-handed. Why couldn't she pick her own hobbies? She went on to explain.

"To be honest, I think he just wanted to distract me from my real passion: amateur dramatics. He gets a bit jealous, especially when I'm playing the love interest or female lead. It's completely unnecessary."

She began to fan herself gently with her passport.

"For example, when I told him that at our last show, in a little village hall, the men and women had to share a dressing room, he went bananas. Honestly, he's got no idea of the practicalities of being on stage."

Slipping her passport under her arm to free both hands, she undid the top two buttons of her low-cut blouse.

"How about you? What do you write?"

I'd already prepared a stock answer.

"Non-fiction, chiefly. I write about plants and gardening for our local magazine, and I'm editing my great-aunt's letters for publication."

"Your aunt? Is she famous? Will I have heard of her?"

I stood up a little straighter, despite the enervating heat that made me want to wilt.

"Probably. May Sayers, the travel writer. She wrote lots of travelogue books and features for the national press."

Lydia shrugged. "Sorry, I don't really read books or newspapers. Has she ever been in *Hello!* magazine?"

I shook my head. Lydia's husband was plummeting in my estimation. What an inappropriate gift he had chosen for her.

An older woman sidled into the gap beside Lydia.

"Sorry, I couldn't help overhearing, but I'm going to the retreat at Hotel Ola Kala too. I'm Cecilia."

We both turned to welcome her and introduce ourselves.

"And what do you write?" we asked in unison, then laughed self-consciously. I was getting flashbacks to the conversations in Freshers' week at uni: "*What A Levels did you do? What grades did you get? What school did you go to?*"

"Contemporary women's fiction," said Cecilia. "Books to empower single women to lead the lives they desire without needing a man."

Lydia giggled. "Too late for me, I'm afraid. I'm a married woman."

"*Echo filo*," I said, remembering Hector's inscription in the Greek phrasebook.

Cecilia's eyes fixed on me. "Is yours Greek?"

"Is who Greek?" asked Lydia. "My husband? No, he's British, like me."

"No, Sophie's boyfriend. She just said in Greek she has a boyfriend."

I grinned apologetically.

"It's the only Greek phrase I know, apart from *kalimera*. My boyfriend, Hector, wrote it in the front of the Greek phrasebook he gave me."

Cecilia scowled. "That's a solid Greek name. Not one of those Mediterranean controlling types, is he?"

Lydia sneaked a conspiratorial smile at me.

"Not remotely. His surname's Scottish: Munro. But he's from the Cotswolds, and it doesn't get much more English than that."

We were spared any further embarrassment by a clunk from the luggage belt and the thud of the first suitcase sliding down the chute to be reunited with its owner. My backpack was almost the last item to arrive, but Lydia and Cecilia stayed with me to keep me company.

Cecilia seemed the most practical of the three of us. "I think we're being sent a taxi to share to the ferry, so no point in going on without you."

We passed swiftly through the customs channel, which I was surprised to find unmanned.

"Probably all still asleep after lunch," observed Cecilia, whose suitcase bore stickers from previous trips to Greece. "No change there then!"

She seemed to know where she was going, not that this airport was big enough to get lost in. Lydia and I followed her through the double doors that marked the point of no return.

"That's us, over there." She nodded towards a tall, sturdily built Greek man in long fawn shorts and a white T-shirt. He held a gleaming tablet at eye level – the electronic kind, I mean, not a Ten Commandments stone type – bearing each of our names in Comic Sans: Lydia Fairfax, Cecilia Fry, Sophie Sayers – and Marina Milanese.

7 A Taxing Ride

A clatter behind us heralded the arrival of Marina through the automatic doors from the customs channel. The captain of our flight was pushing a trolley piled high with designer luggage, her vanity case nestling coquettishly beside his black pilot's case. Marina spotted our taxi driver's tablet and directed the pilot to steer the trolley across to us.

"Bit late for the Mile-High Club now," Cecilia murmured to Lydia and me. "Too old for it as well."

The captain seized his case, turned the trolley's handle towards the taxi driver, and stepped back to offer Marina a smart farewell salute. Cecilia, Lydia and I didn't hesitate to pile our baggage on top of Marina's. At Lydia's sweet smile of silent appeal, the driver grabbed the trolley's handle with authority and spoke in a rich, gravelly voice.

"OK, let us be on our way. Ladies, please follow me."

"Nice tablet," said Marina, walking beside him while the rest of us followed behind. "I had expected a handwritten cardboard sign."

The driver narrowed his eyes at her.

"You think we are backwards in Greece? We are not. We were civilised long before you."

Marina smiled as if he'd paid her a compliment. Did she not understand, or was she just not listening?

He led us to the car park where his large and gleaming black Mercedes awaited us. He opened the doors, and when Marina went to sit in the back seat, he held up his hand to stop her.

"No, you go in front, please, missus. The girls go in back. You need space."

Again, Marina smiled, interpreting his comment as a mark of respect. If she'd seen him wink at the three of us behind her back, she'd have realised he meant she was fat, although she wasn't. Well, not very.

Once he'd stored our luggage in the boot, he slid into the driver's seat and started the near-silent engine. Soon we were on the exit road, then driving through countryside dotted with orange and olive trees, wild herbs and grasses. A gust of chilled air swept through the car, the air-conditioning on full blast. When Marina shivered dramatically, he tapped the dashboard.

"Is good, yes? While everyone else too hot, Kostas's car is cool. I am cool."

He beamed at us via the rear-view mirror for so long that I worried about his focus on the road. He averted his gaze from us only when his mobile phone rang. Slipping the latest iPhone out of his shirt pocket, he gazed at the screen, then clicked "*Accept call*". There followed a barrage of heated conversation, with Kostas driving one-handed. The only words I could identify, having perused the phrasebook on the plane, were *ne* and *oxi*, which I hadn't yet quite got to grips with. *Ne* sounds more like no than yes, and *oxi* sounds like OK but means no. No wonder I'm confused.

When he eventually hung up, via the rear-view mirror he re-established eye contact with the three of us on the back seat.

"Just my mama asking what I want to eat tonight."

Then, as if he didn't care to have both hands on the wheel when only one would suffice, he picked up a pack of cigarettes from the dashboard and tapped one out into his mouth.

Marina coughed in protest before he'd even lit it. I thought it best to distract her.

"Look, Marina, is this Argostoli already? It's where they filmed *Captain Corelli's Mandolin*."

I'd not read the book, but Hector thought it was better than the film. I wished I'd brought it with me to read now. The modern buildings and the line of market stalls selling beach towels and sun hats surprised me.

"No, no, this resort is a recent development," said Cecilia. "You'll see a lot of modern buildings on both Kefalonia and Ithaca after so much was destroyed by the terrible 1953 earthquake. All that Venetian beauty ruined. The revamped centre of Argostoli is very smart, with its polished marble pavements, but classical architecture it ain't."

That pleased Kostas.

"You've been to Kefalonia before? You know about our history?"

"Yes. Many times. All around the Ionian islands, in fact – Kefalonia, Ithaca, Lefkas, Zakynthos. But my heart lies in Ithaca."

"Kefalonia is better," asserted Kostas.

As we drove into the capital, then across the causeway and up the winding road signposting Mount Aenos, he began a running commentary of the highlights.

"You built this causeway for us. British always welcome on Kefalonia."

As we reached the edge of the pine forest, he opened all the windows and breathed deeply.

"Kefalonia pine. Only in Kefalonia. Kefalonia is best."

The three of us in the back inhaled great gasps of air and made appreciative noises. Marina closed her window back up.

Eventually we descended towards the little harbour town of Sami, gleaming white and cerulean blue, dazzling against the glistening sea. The harbour wall was edged in canopied bars and restaurants with stunning views across the water to Ithaca. Ithaca, home to Homer and Odysseus, and the birthplace of story: how could we fail to be inspired in such a legendary setting – or daunted by its rich heritage?

Kostas decanted us and our luggage at the ferry terminal, then took his leave, his bill paid in advance by the retreat's organiser.

"I'm glad we got here in one piece," said Marina, watching the black Mercedes glinting in the sun as it ascended the hill. "Any British taxi driver who took phone calls at the wheel would lose his licence in no time."

Her criticism washed over Lydia.

"Well, I thought he was a very nice man. Very informative. What beautiful trees. I'd like to paint that mountain. Besides, he didn't crash the car, did he? He knew what he was doing. There's not much traffic and he must know the roads as well as anybody."

Cecilia huffed. "Yes, just like all the Greek drivers who plunge off cliffs and into the sea, or steer into other vehicles or pedestrians. Didn't you notice all the shrines along the way?"

I'd been wondering about the little white boxes on stilts, full of lit candles and icons.

"I found them rather charming," I said. "The local people must be very devout around here to have a place of worship every mile or two."

Cecilia pursed her lips. "Those shrines are all memorials, put up by bereaved mothers and wives grieving for the loss of their reckless menfolk driving motorbikes or cars."

These islands were more dangerous than I'd imagined.

"Do you know this area well?" Marina sounded resentful that one of us might have an advantage over her.

Cecilia paused before replying. "I spent many summers here in my younger days."

Lydia perked up.

"Ooh, did you have any good holiday romances? Is that what you write about?" At last we seemed to have alighted upon the kind of book that Lydia might read.

Cecilia hesitated.

"I don't write romance. That would be more up your street, Marina."

"But never mind what you write, Cecilia, how many holiday romances did you have?" Lydia clapped her hands. "Do tell! You never know, Marina, Cecilia could give you ideas for your next blockbuster."

Marina's face was solemn. "Beware. All writers are jackdaws. Don't tell me your secrets unless you're happy for them to resurface in one of my novels. As a professional author –" she emphasised "professional", as if ranking the rest of us as amateurs – "I cannot be responsible for my actions for the sake of a good story."

She fixed her gaze on Cecilia.

"In that case, don't blame me if I push you off the Ithaca ferry," said Cecilia, turning away.

"That won't spare you," retorted Marina. "I'm a very strong swimmer. Probably better than any of you."

Was there anything she didn't feel superior about?

8 All Afloat

Once on the ferry to Ithaca, we piled our luggage together, then took turns to stroll around the deck. The views were the most beautiful I'd ever seen, even more dramatic than the Scottish Highlands and Islands. The refreshing breeze quickly dispersed any weariness, and the calm sea twinkled hypnotically.

Halfway across the channel, a pod of dolphins, as if sent by the Greek Tourist Board to enhance our experience, gambolled alongside the ferry, playing up to the click of our cameras. Marina turned her back on the dolphins to take selfies with them. The only passengers unmoved by the spectacle were the locals, who spent the whole journey gossiping in the cool and shady bar below deck.

Our voyage, unlike Odysseus's, was over all too quickly. Within the hour we found ourselves on the harbourside at Vathy, our luggage stacked beside us. As the other foot passengers from the ferry were scooped up by various trucks, cars, motor scooters and, in one case, a wooden donkey cart, by a process of attrition, we were left with three strangers who turned out to be our fellow delegates.

A young man drew up beside us in a dusty white minibus, stepped down from the cab and held up another tablet. This time we had to squint to see our names, and not only because of the bright sunshine. The print was small to fit in three more names beneath ours – Dawn Wells, Tristram DeVere and Ben Johnstone. Ben's byline was familiar from the arts pages of national newspapers, but I'd never seen his name on a book at Hector's House.

After piling our bags into the back of the minibus, we climbed aboard. I slid into the third row of seats, with Ben and Dawn following. In the second row sat Cecilia and Marina, with Lydia sandwiched between Tristram and the driver on the front seat.

"I'll never remember everyone's names," said Lydia, twisting around to bestow her smile upon us all.

"No worries," said the driver in a strong Australian twang, starting the engine and pulling out onto the main road along the seafront. "You won't have to remember many more. Where we're going there is just me, my mother Katerina, and my grandmother, Ariadne, in the village shop. And my father when he is home from the mainland. Oh, and a load of old monks, but you'll never see them. They keep themselves to themselves."

"But what's your name?" asked Lydia, beaming up at him. "You haven't told us your name yet."

He grinned down at her.

"I am Vasili."

"Vasili?" said Cecilia behind him in a voice that suggested it was the most extraordinary name she'd ever heard. Perhaps, like me, she was surprised at the dissonance between his antipodean accent and his Greek name.

He nodded as if accustomed to having his name queried.

"Short for Vasilios, like my father. Not so strange to your English ear when you know that a Greek V is a little like an English B. Which turns my name into Basil where you come from. We're all named after saints here, you know."

Lydia laughed as she prodded him in the ribs.

"So you're the island's equivalent of Basil Fawlty. That's hysterical."

She seemed easily amused.

"There are plenty of people here," said Ben. "And plenty of houses and bars and shops. Surely they're not all day trippers?"

Many of them looked Greek. I guessed this must be a popular holiday resort for Greeks as well as foreign tourists.

"Sure, mate," said Vasili, returning a friendly wave from a passer-by. "But this is the mainland. Where you're going is a tiny island that's fallen off the end of Ithaca. Floros, it's called. And you're bunking down at the Hotel Ola Kala, which is run by Mum and me. I'm just driving you to Frikes were my boat is parked."

"The mainland?" queried Dawn, whose face and voice I recognised from a popular writing vlog. "But Ithaca's an island. Everybody knows that."

Vasili shrugged. "Hey, it's all relative, babe. Some folk would say Australia's an island. A bloody big one, but indisputably an island. Compare it to Tasmania, and it's mainland. You get me?"

"Are you Australian, Vasili?" asked Dawn.

"Hell, no. But I spent some time there when I was a kid. Learned English and stuff, then came home. To Floros."

41

There was a moment's silence while the news sank in that the retreat wasn't on Ithaca after all. I regretted that we wouldn't have a chance to explore this lively seafront.

"Isn't that a bit of a con?" asked Tristram, folding his arms across his chest. "I mean, we've been sold a week on Ithaca. We could have you under the Trades Descriptions Act."

Vasili shrugged. "Not here, this is Greece. But if you ask me, Floros is the better place for a writing retreat. You'll have none of the hustle and bustle of a touristy place like Vathy. Floros has all the advantages of Ithaca without the crowds or the yachties, apart from the day trippers on the excursion boat from Lefkas, but that's only once a day for a couple of hours and they can seldom be bothered to climb the hill up to our hotel."

He rubbed his tummy, making me realise I was hungry.

"Plus, you get my mama's cooking, and she is the best! You'll love it, I promise you. Just you wait and see!"

When I saw his tiny wooden fishing boat waiting to ferry us from Frikes to Floros, I wasn't so sure.

9 All Adrift

Marina picked her way between the bare plank seats to the best one right at the front. For some reason, we'd all stood aside to let her go first. When she leaned forward, figurehead style, to take a selfie, I feared she might drop her phone into the sea.

"I read somewhere that the poet Byron used to swim off Ithaca," said Ben as he clambered aboard. "I've been doing some background reading on the area in preparation for this retreat. Did you realise we're following in the footsteps of Byron as well as Homer?"

"Didn't Byron drown out here?" The Romantics module of my English A Level was starting to come back to me. Ben settled down beside me on the second plank seat from the back.

"You're thinking of Shelley," said Cecilia. "And that was on an Italian lake in a thunderstorm. Byron died during the Greek wars of independence. He's still considered a local hero."

I laughed. "You could make a good variant of my favourite board game featuring interesting deaths of poets. Christopher Marlowe, with the knife, in the bar."

"Socrates, with the hemlock, in the prison cell," said Dawn, entering into the spirit of the game. "Does he count as a poet?"

"Of course not, he was a philosopher, and besides, you've got the whole concept wrong," snapped Marina. "In the board game the characters are the murderers, not the victims."

I was about to defend myself by emphasising that this should be a variant, not a slavish copy, but didn't want to antagonise her further.

Ben leaned back to gaze up at the cloudless blue sky, sliding his arms along the edge of the boat until one of them brushed my shoulder. "I don't think we'll have to worry about storms here, will we, Vasili?"

In my head I thanked him for glossing over my error.

Vasili was reeling in the rope that had secured the boat to a steel ring sunk into the harbour wall.

"No storms on our agenda for you, mate."

He wound the rope into a neat coil before stowing it in a wooden locker beneath the back seat.

Lydia was undaunted by any talk of storms and drowning.

"Are there any decent beaches on this Floros place?"

Vasili bent down to start the motor, but remained standing throughout the crossing, his hand on the tiller.

"Sorry, love, only stony ones for you."

As soon as the motor had jolted into life, we began to move slowly out into the bay, Vasili's hand firm on the tiller. "But at least you don't have to worry about getting sand in your bikini." He took his eyes off the horizon to wink at Lydia. "The only sandy beach on Floros is the preserve of the monks."

"Monks?" Lydia giggled. "Why do monks need a beach?"

Vasili shrugged. "Same as the rest of us. They get hot and sticky, fancy a bathe, to get back to nature, that sort of thing. I think their need is greater than yours, given their dress code." He looked her up and down.

I'd noticed a Greek Orthodox priest on the boat from Kefalonia, with thick curly salt-and-pepper hair and a long beard. Beneath his tall black hat and long robe, he must have been baking. No wonder he'd headed downstairs to the shady bar as soon as he'd boarded.

Lydia, perched on the locker, eyed Vasili's sturdy bare calves.

"So, where do you go to cool down on Floros?"

"Our hotel has the best swimming pool on the island. I spend a lot of time in the pool myself, when I get the chance."

Tiring of being a figurehead, Marina turned to stare wistfully back towards Ithaca.

"I'm guessing it's the only swimming pool on Floros," she said.

Vasili gave her a lop-sided grin.

"Too right, sweetheart. Unless the monks have one tucked away that I don't know about."

Marina was not amused.

"I was promised a free week on Ithaca, not on a lump of rock that had fallen off the end."

Tristram frowned. "What do you mean, free? Did you not pay for it like the rest of us?"

Marina gave him a reproving look. "My dear, I'm part of the deal for you. I am the bestselling novelist you were promised as part of your package. In return for my free stay, I waive my usual speaker's fee. So really, you're getting a bargain. An inspiration and fount of wisdom for paying delegates. I am a cost of sale, as a businessman like you might put it."

"Or woman. Or businesswoman," said Cecilia.

Tristram leaned forward, his hands on his knees. "Let me get this straight. What you're saying is you are here on a freebie to make the course more attractive to the rest of us."

"And more valuable."

"You mean more expensive," returned Dawn. "There are eight of us on this course, but now seven of us are being charged an eighth of your flight, board and lodging to give you a free holiday?"

I tried to change the direction of the conversation, hoping none of them knew my place was also free.

"So, Dawn, Tristram, what sort of business are you two in?"

Dawn and Tristram looked at each other in alarm, then laughed.

"We're not in business together, Sophie, nor are we an item, if that's what you're thinking," said Tristram. "We just happened to fly in on the same plane from Gatwick. I don't know about you, Dawn, but I'm what you might term a serial entrepreneur. I set up businesses, build 'em up and sell them on."

"Don't I know it," murmured Ben.

When Tristram looked startled, Ben explained.

"I used to be a business reporter until I moved across to the arts. You won't have seen my byline in the business pages as in those days I was too junior, but I've written the odd story about your various ventures, Tristram. And I've read about yours, Dawn. Your work as an entrepreneur and an author straddles both my areas of interest."

"An authorpreneur." Dawn drew herself up primly.

That was a new term for me. "What's one of those?" I asked.

"Someone who treats their writing like a business, developing multiple income streams via podcasts, merchandise, courses, and so on."

Tristram held up his hands. "Whoa! Not for me. I just want to write my memoir. I see it as a kind of 80,000-word business card, a good advertisement for all I do, and an altruistic gesture to aspiring entrepreneurs who want to emulate my success."

"We're not disagreeing," said Dawn.

Lydia pouted.

"But I don't want to run a business. My husband said writing would just be a hobby. I didn't know he was training me up to work for my living."

Cecilia gave a hollow laugh. "Yes, God forbid you might have to work for your living."

Vasili steered a sharp right, then left, making us all fall sideways and bump into each other – a clever tactic to cut the squabble short.

"Don't stress, guys. I am sure whatever you are hoping to get out of this week, you will find satisfaction."

"Like a free holiday," muttered Dawn, but before Marina could respond, we were pulling into a small bay on the tiny island of Floros and mooring alongside a sun-bleached wooden jetty at right angles to the stony beach.

To my surprise, after what Vasili had said about the limited population, another boat was already moored there – a smart sailing yacht about twelve metres long. Stepping ashore was a fresh-faced young blond man with a light tan.

"Bye, Pa." He gave a brief wave to an equally handsome man a generation ahead of him. "See you in a week."

"Bye, chap." His father had the forced indifference of one who thought any outward show of affection to a boy child was a sign of weakness in them both. "Stay sober and keep it in your pants."

I thought the young man's pants was an odd place to keep alcohol, but I wasn't about to add my twopenn'orth to the paternal counsel. To my relief, this new arrival looked more affable than some other members of our party. He'd lighten the mood in no time. As Vasili secured our boat to the jetty, he bounded along the shaky boards towards us with the energy of a tawny Labrador puppy.

"Hey, guys, are you all on this retreat thing too? Ace!"

He cast his eyes eagerly over Lydia and me, as if trying to choose which of us to have first.

"Hello, girls, I'm Dominic, but you can call me Dom, like James Bond's favourite champagne."

His smile was warm and genuine as he reached down with both hands to help Lydia and me climb out of the boat. With impeccable manners, he did the same for Dawn and Marina, and would have done for Cecilia had she not rebuffed his offer by stuffing her hands into her pockets.

The splash of an anchor creaking on its chain as it was hauled up from the water signalled the impending departure of Dominic's father's yacht.

"Sorry if Pa seems a bit abrupt, sloping off like that, but he wants to take advantage of the five o'clock blow to reach Fiskardo for the night."

That meant nothing to most of us.

"The five o'clock blow?" I queried.

Dominic grinned. "Very obliging weather in these parts. Winds as regular as clockwork. Not worth setting sail till ten in the morning as there's no wind to speak of. Calm by seven, with a last boost around five giving just enough puff to see you into your evening berth. That's why the Ionian is so popular for sailing. Pa says it's lazy and the equivalent of the nursery slopes in skiing, but I love it."

So, he spent his summers sailing and his winters skiing. What a great source of material for a writer. It made life in Wendlebury Barrow seem a bit tame.

Vasili finished unloading our luggage on to the jetty.

"Guys, I'm sorry but you'll have to carry your own bags to the hotel. We don't have vehicles on Floros."

Marina groaned. "My God, it gets more primitive by the minute."

"Except for you, Miss Milanese." Vasili winked at the rest of us. "Allow me."

Carrying all four of her bags, he led the way across the stony beach and up a gently sloping dirt track. At the top stood a wide two-storey building, the walls painted a warm orange, the shutters a deep blue. The white wrought-iron balconies were softened by the embrace of cerise bougainvillea. Its perfume drifted down to greet us, mingling agreeably with the fresh sea breeze and astringent wild herbs fringing the path. Now that we were on dry land, I became aware of a gentle chorus of chirruping in the background. Presumably these were the famous cicadas.

I glanced at my watch: five o'clock Greek time, three o'clock in Wendlebury Barrow. The children would just be coming out of the village school. Hector seemed a very long way away.

Lydia stepped out alongside Dominic, who had shouldered his sailing duffel bag to free his hands for her suitcase.

"At last. Away from it all!" she squealed, dancing alongside him like an excited child.

It crossed my mind that for Lydia, 'it' might mean the watchful eye of her husband.

10 Xenophilia

Although the afternoon heat was waning now, Vasili was wilting beneath the weight of Marina's many bags as we climbed up the slope. Carrying only a clutch bag, Marina picked her way along the rough path so as not to get dust on her sugar-pink velvet wedge sandals. A gentle breeze teased my loose hair, presumably Dominic's five o'clock blow drifting up from the sea.

A woman in her forties with dark curls drawn back into a ponytail came down the path to meet us.

"Welcome to the Hotel Ola Kala!"

She made a beeline for Marina.

"Miss Milanese! I am so honoured to meet you; I have all your books. I never miss one."

"Hello to you too," muttered Cecilia from the back of our procession.

"I am Katerina," the woman continued in her soft Greek accent. "I am the owner and manager of the hotel, so if there is anything you need during your stay, please come to me and ask me. Or my son, Vasili. Vasili! Vasili!" She called to make sure he was paying attention, then turned back to Marina. "Vasili will run the hotel when I am gone. But not for a long time yet, if it pleases God. At least not while you are here, ha ha! But you have had a long journey. You are tired. Let us check you in. Vasili will take your bags to your rooms while you have a glass of our local wine. My mama, she makes all our wine from our grapes on the hill there." She waved her arm towards a neatly planted vineyard on a slope behind the hotel. "It is very good. Now, Vasili, Vasili, hurry! He is a lazy boy." She rolled her eyes. "But one day, when I am gone, he will work hard."

Of all of us, Vasili looked most in need of a restorative glass of his grandmother's wine.

"So, we go." Katerina raised her right hand in the air to lead us, but with only one building in sight – if you didn't count a tall, tumbledown windmill, its sails in shreds, on the next hill along – we could hardly have got lost.

I was glad I'd brought my backpack rather than a suitcase, enabling me to walk faster than the others and catch up with Katerina.

"What's that up there?" I pointed to the ruin.

"Ah, this is the old windmill. For the olive oil. My mama, she still makes it, but we take the olives to the monastery now. The big earthquake in 1953 – you heard of this? – it damaged the windmill, and it has never been repaired. Many people left Floros after earthquake. They like the water, the gas, the electric there and don't come back."

She shrugged at their disloyalty.

"But my mama, she stay. Her mama and baba buried here and she not want to leave. I do not think Vasili will be that way with me. But if I keep hotel good for him, he have own business when I die and he stay."

(Baba was Greek for dad, my phrase book told me later.)

Katerina glanced back at Vasili as he staggered to join us on the threshold of the hotel, where the wrought iron gates were already thrown wide in welcome, the marble steps softened by numerous pots of scarlet geraniums and dusky grey-green herbs.

"Slowly he learn."

She propped open the double doors and beckoned us through to the hotel lobby. This shady room, cooled by marble floors, was lined with wicker chairs, into which we all now collapsed, thankful for the evening breeze that followed us in. Katerina bustled behind the counter, producing registration forms.

"I'm sorry, I trust you, but it is the law. The hotel police, they angry if we don't do."

"The hotel police?" Ben pulled a pad and pencil from the pocket of his flight bag and started to scribble in shorthand. "You have hotel police on Floros? That seems overkill for such a tiny population. Where do they live? In the hotel or with the monks? Surely you don't have an island police station?"

Katerina waved her hand in dismissal. "No, no, there are no police on the island, apart from my husband, Vasili's father, and he is only on the island on his days off. He works on mainland."

"That's a long way to commute for a day off, poor bloke," said Tristram. "It must be two ferries at least, plus a drive? I think there is a mainland ferry from Ithaca, is it to Poros or Piraeus?"

"To Floros, Ithaca seems like the mainland," I reminded him.

Katerina nodded.

"My husband, he work on Ithaca. That is not so far. And Vasili, he fetch him in his boat. Personal water-taxi pilot."

She smiled fondly at Vasili. A lot of tasks seemed to fall under his job description.

One by one, Katerina assigned us room numbers and gave us keys. The rooms had been left unlocked to allow Vasili to deliver our bags. There was no lift. We watched him stumble on the stairs under the weight of Marina's luggage.

"What on earth have you got in there, Marina?" asked Ben, his pen poised over his notepad. "Do you always take a dead body on holiday with you?"

Marina gave a rippling laugh. "My books, of course. I never travel without a complete set, and there are forty-three of them now. Plus a dozen of my latest. You never know when you might meet a fan who wants to buy a signed copy."

Cecilia, out of Marina's sight in an alcove, made a retching motion.

Lydia's brow creased with worry.

"But hang on, if you're that successful already, haven't you got better things to do than be here?"

Marina smiled indulgently.

"My dear, as a writer one should always be learning." Lydia looked even more worried. "As well as being here to give you the benefit of my experience, as I mentioned before, I may learn something myself. I keep an open mind. I'm not just a bestselling romantic novelist. I have plans, you know – but they are all under wraps just now. I must say no more. And of course, I may make new friends."

She made eyes at Tristram, who was at least ten years younger than her, and he flinched.

"Plans, eh?" said Ben, his reporter's instincts aroused. "I'd love to have a one-to-one chat with you sometime about the notion of changing genres. It could make a great exclusive for my paper, when you launch your next book."

Marina looked at her watch. "You must ask my agent." Then she turned her attention to Katerina. "What does a girl have to do to get a drink around here?"

"Vasili!" His mother called up the stairs, where he had just taken the final pieces of luggage. "Our guests are thirsty. And meanwhile, Miss Milanese, I like to show you the little library I have assembled for hotel guests."

She opened a pair of dove-grey louvre doors to reveal a cupboard fitted floor-to-ceiling with bookshelves. The top three held novels in English, the rest had books in other languages. One of the English language shelves was devoted to books by Marina Milanese. Katerina pointed proudly.

"You see, we are big fans. Please, you sign them while you are our guest? It would mean a lot to me and to all my guests. If anyone cannot decide what to read, I always recommend your books"

"None of mine in translation, I notice." Marina scanned the foreign language shelves and sighed. "I'm sorry, Katerina, my agent insists I only sign books at the point of purchase so as not to devalue my autograph. I'm sure you understand."

Katerina's lips tightened into a straight line.

"I get wine."

As she exited through the swing door behind the reception desk, I couldn't help but wonder why Marina was being so hostile towards her host for the next week, especially when she'd willingly signed a book for a fellow passenger on the flight over. I wasn't the only one to be perplexed.

Tristram looked disdainful

"If I were you, Marina, I'd change your agent. Her grasping attitude may have just lost you a fan and an energetic advocate. Word-of-mouth recommendation is the best advertising any business can have."

"I'm not a business," retorted Marina. "I'm an author. An artiste."

"You're a business," put in a new voice. "Believe me, you're a business."

"What do you know about it?"

That was a rude way for Marina to welcome the newcomer. The woman, blonde, slim, smartly dressed and in her late thirties, slipped into the only empty chair, beside Tristram.

"If you're not a business, how come you've got an agent?" he asked Marina. "Just to wangle free trips for you?"

"Well, it's better to get the whole trip free than set the cost against tax," returned Marina.

"I rest my case," said Tristram, with a smirk. Then he turned to the late arrival. "I'm sorry, we haven't been introduced. I'm Tristram DeVere. I'm here to progress my memoir. How about you?"

The woman smiled at his courtesy. "I'm Kimberley Houston. I'm here to kick start my first novel. I got stuck at twenty thousand words about three years ago and can't move forward. I just keep editing what I've already written. I thought a focussed week in the company of other writers would help."

"Saggy middle," declared Marina, keen to reassert her authority. "A common enough problem in beginners."

All eyes shot to Kimberley's abdomen, which was taut as the top of a newly-opened jar of jam. Marina threw back her head and laughed with the self-assurance of a kookaburra.

"In your manuscript, I mean. Well, I can tell you without even looking at it where you're going wrong. Editing and writing are two different parts of the brain. Dash your first draft off to get your story on the page. Only then go back and edit. Otherwise you'll be taking your unfinished manuscript to your grave."

She glanced around at all of our faces to check we were hanging on her every word. Albeit reluctantly, we were.

"And you wonder why they gave me a free place on the retreat? Surely I'm proving my value as the voice of experience already."

A week of tension like this wouldn't help anyone.

"To be honest, I'd never heard of you before we arrived today," said Dominc. "But when Katerina came down to meet our boat earlier and got chatting to my dad about the course, I discovered my stepmother's addicted to your books. She likes ebooks. Good for life aboard a boat, they take up less room. Better a tablet than drugs, is my dad's corny joke."

"I'll take that as a compliment, thank you, Dominic."

"Oh, she still takes drugs too. But Pa says your ebooks help get her through the day between the actual tablets."

The swing door squeaked, and Katerina reappeared, bearing a tray loaded with carafes of dark red and pale gold wine and numerous thick stemless glass tumblers. She set the tray down on the coffee table.

"Here is wine for you all. Please help yourselves and tell me when you need more. There is plenty. Mama always makes much wine. The monks, they let her use their press. We pray in their church and they are kind to her."

She didn't look at Marina, apparently still smarting about the autographs.

"Then when you are ready, you eat. We have buffet in dining room through that door." She pointed behind us. "Vasili will be here if you need anything. I go bake now for breakfast."

After we'd filled our glasses, Vasili followed us into the dining room with the tray of carafes. I found myself seated between Kimberley and Ben.

I turned to Kimberley.

"So, you arrived on an earlier flight?" This was stating the obvious, but I wanted to make it clear to Kimberley that I was friendly. "Did you have a good flight?"

Kimberley offered a basket of crusty white bread and butter to me before taking some herself.

"Yes, my flight got in very early. I flew from Edinburgh in the middle of the night. I took the public bus from the airport to Sami, then Vasili met me at Vathy and brought me the rest of the way in his minibus and boat."

A sudden thought struck me.

"I wonder why he leaves his minibus on Ithaca? Doesn't he need it when he gets back to Floros?"

Kimberley shrugged. "There are no roads here, apparently, just dirt tracks. When the island was more or less abandoned after the earthquake in 1953, there were very few vehicles here anyway, and the authorities never got around to repairing the roads or making new ones. If you want to go anywhere on Floros, you have to walk. In Athens they say visiting here is like going back seventy years."

"A bit like visiting the Isle of Wight," said Dawn with a fond smile.

"Oh well, at least we don't have to worry about traffic noise disturbing our muse," said Lydia brightly. "It's the perfect romantic retreat, don't you think, Dom?"

Her eyes glistened as she fixed him with a smile. I was beginning to wonder whether either of them would get any writing done this week.

"Muse? There's no such thing as a muse." Marina drained her second glass of red. "Successful writers just apply themselves and get on with it."

"I wouldn't say that in Greece if I were you, Marina." A new voice joined the conversation from the doorway, belonging to a plump woman with red curls and green eyes. Her light kaftan echoed the colour of the sea we'd just crossed. "Every time you say you don't believe in muses, one of them dies."

Everyone laughed except Marina.

As the newcomer drew out the last empty chair and made herself comfortable on it, the kaftan's loose fabric, patterned with orderly rows of leaping dolphins, fell like waves around her.

She noticed my admiring gaze. "Like it? I bought it this morning from Kat's mum's shop. Just the ticket for coping with Greek heat. She has sarongs in the same pattern too."

She glanced around the table to bring everyone else into the conversation.

"I'm Stacey, by the way, Stacey Sydney. I'm the retreat director. I'll be leading the course over the coming week. I'm really excited to see the fruits of your labour."

I was glad she was confident that there'd be a harvest.

"But we'll leave the formal business till tomorrow. Tonight let's just get to know each other."

Lydia edged her chair a little closer to Dominic's, and Ben, on the pretext of stretching his arms, laid one gently along the back of my chair. I shifted forward on my seat to evade his touch.

Stacey waved her hand across the fine array of dishes. I had yet to learn their names, but they filled the room with a savoury, herby fragrance. "Let's eat, drink, and be merry," she said. "For tomorrow we write."

11 After Dark

Night had fallen by the time we'd finished eating. Only then did I realise I hadn't texted Hector since we landed at Kefalonia Airport. Not that I'd promised to phone him with any particular frequency. He wasn't keeping tabs on me. I just wanted to.

As Vasili brought us all coffees, I pulled out my phone and tapped the short code for Hector's flat. I couldn't even raise a dialling tone.

Vasili set a cup of fragrant black coffee down in front of me.

"No mobile signal here, sweetheart."

"Where in the hotel can I get one?"

"Nowhere, love, sorry. It's not worth any phone company's while to install a transmitter on Floros just for us and our guests."

Marina tuned into our conversation. "Does this mean you don't have wi-fi in the hotel?"

"No, mate."

Marina bridled at the expression.

"What about the monastery?"

She was rather clutching at straws now.

Vasili laughed and slapped his thigh. "Yeah, those monks like to get in their daily game of Words with Friends. Strewth, love, half the time they don't even speak."

Cecilia raised her eyebrows.

"I thought all Greek people loved their mobile phones? Last time I was here, I was told that Greece had the highest concentration of mobile phones in the world."

Vasili grinned.

"Well, keeping the tiny population of Floros incommunicado will hardly make a dent in those figures. Anyway, aren't you guys here for a retreat? You don't want to go distracting yourselves with internet garbage."

Lydia paused her tête-à-tête with Dominic.

"But I need to phone my husband."

Dominic removed his hand from her thigh.

"Every day and every night. Or at least text him. He'll be worried if I don't."

"I'd like to phone my boyfriend too," I said, glad to make it clear to Ben that I wasn't single. *Echo filo.*

Vasili's face softened.

"Well, if you really want to call them, you can just about get a signal up by the windmill."

"Just about?" Marina's face was stern. "Just about isn't good enough. I need a strong enough signal to upload photos every day to my social media pages. And I haven't uploaded any that I took on your little boat."

Vasili grinned again.

"Quite the Kate Winslet there, weren't you?"

Marina took this as a compliment. Vasili polled the table.

"Anyone else have an urgent need to contact their fans tonight?"

Cecilia shook her head vehemently.

"I've left all my admin to my VA," said Dawn.

Dominic sat back in his chair and set down his cutlery on his plate. "What's a VA? Sounds like some kind of disease."

Dawn looked ever so slightly smug. "Virtual assistant. Like a PA but in a remote location. I send her instructions over the internet."

Tristram nodded approval. "Sound strategy. The internet allows you to use the services of anyone anywhere in the world, and to get a more competitive rate than in your home country. No overheads for you to carry, either. I wish I could get away with that. I pay my PA in London an extortionate amount."

Vasili waved his hand to summon Marina, Lydia and me to follow him. "Come on then, ladies, I'll take you up the hill now so you can each say goodnight to your sweetheart. Or sweethearts in your case, Marina. We don't want your thousands of adoring fans losing sleep if you don't report in with a late-night selfie. But be careful, the path is treacherous in the dark. Anyone want to change their shoes first?"

As Marina got up from her seat, he looked pointedly at her velvet wedges.

"Oh, for goodness' sake, I'm perfectly comfortable in these. Let's just go."

She stumbled slightly as one of her shoes turned on its side, but that was possibly due to the empty wine carafe by her plate rather than her choice of footwear. She'd emptied a whole carafe of red on her own.

Cecilia sniggered.

***

63

Vasili's torch wasn't really necessary. The nearly full moon shone brightly in the cloudless skies.

Lydia gasped.

"Wow! Look at all those stars! You've got a lot more stars than we have in England."

Vasili grinned. "We have the same number as you, silly. We just don't have your light pollution to stop us seeing them. And if you like this, you should try the night skies in the Australian outback. They'd take your breath away."

"I've heard that before," I said. Hector's twin brother Horace had charmed me with tales of his adventures down under. We'd first met at their parents' house in Clevedon on the tame Somerset coast with its opaque steel grey sea.

The uneven path was beset with small, loose rocks that slipped underfoot. Fortunately, it was also demarcated on the left by low shrubs, and to the right the glossy needles on a row of tall pine trees gleamed in the moonlight. We trudged after Vasili in silence, concentrating on keeping our footing. Only once did I reach out sideways to stop myself falling and had the bad luck to grasp a branch covered in thorns.

Finally, the path levelled out on to a summit, at the far side of which stood the ruined windmill, eerie in the moonlight. I strolled as close as I dared – which was not very close – towards the edge of the cliff to admire the view.

"Crikey, you're brave, Sophie," exclaimed Lydia. "Bob would go mad if I took a risk like that." She'd stopped, wide-eyed, at the top of the path.

"Never mind what he thinks," said Marina. "Let's just get on with what we came here for and get back down for a nightcap."

Perhaps she secretly found her muse in the bottle.

As soon as she found a signal, Marina began sharing photos taken on the journey on her various social media platforms. Lydia called Bob, loudly declaring her safe arrival and undying love at length and with passion. She had clearly mastered voice projection at her amateur dramatics group. I preferred to keep my exchange with Hector private, typing a quick text and immediately receiving a warm reply. He must have been watching his phone, hoping to hear from me. The clock on my phone told me it was ten o'clock Greek time, which would be eight in Wendlebury Barrow. I followed up with a PS to look out of his window at the beautiful moon, and to know I was looking at the same one.

"*Cloudy night in WB,*" he replied. "*Moon's done a bunk but appreciate sentiment. Got far with The Odyssey yet? Homer xxx*"

I bit my lip. I was on page 3.

"*Loving it. Penelope xxx*"

I planned to be more forthcoming in my travel journal.

12 What's Your Motivation?

Lydia leaned towards Ben at the breakfast table. "Sophie was awfully brave last night. Brave and reckless."

Ben looked up from his omelette. "Not skinny-dipping in the Med at midnight?"

Dominic drizzled honey on to thick set yoghurt in his small pottery bowl. "It's the Ionian Sea here, actually."

"Oh yes, of course." Ben jotted it down in his notebook, which lay on the table beside his coffee cup.

"So, were you skinny-dipping?" Dom may have been asking me, but his eyes were on Lydia.

"I think what Lydia means is that I dared to go within three metres of the cliff edge. Hardly courageous."

Dominic chuckled. "You're easily impressed, Lydia. But that suits me!"

Ben looked up from his notepad. "What are the cliffs like round here? Do they crumble easily?"

His question made me wonder whether I'd been more reckless than I thought. Dominic's answer put me at my ease.

"They're not like the White Cliffs of Dover, if that's what you mean. Pure volcanic rock, sturdy as you like. You get the odd rock fall, but not great chunks of ground falling away under your feet." He turned to Marina, who was spreading ivory butter over a thick slice of crusty milk-white bread. "Your selfies will get through, Miss Milanese. Your fans need have no fear."

"Still, I won't hang around up there when I'm phoning Bob in future," said Lydia, caressing a fuzzy-skinned peach. "If I tell him it's unsafe, he won't mind."

"If he's such a worrier, won't he tell you not to phone at all?" I asked.

She stared at me for a moment, as if wondering what to say.

"Oh no," she said at last. "Oh no, he'd never say that." She returned the peach to the fruit bowl.

***

I was the first to arrive at the venue for our writing sessions, a vine-covered wooden pergola beside the pool. When Lydia sat down beside me, I was still trying to get the last of the breakfast honey off my fingertips. Despite washing my hands three times with the olive oil soap in my en-suite bathroom, they were still sticky; I felt like a high-sugar version of Lady Macbeth.

On the low table before us Vasili set down four large jugs of iced water and ten chilled glasses, beaded with condensation. Stacey, as course leader, and Marina, as special guest, were to sit in bigger chairs than the rest of us, like rattan thrones with arms, while ours were white plastic stackables.

His duties finished for the morning, Vasili peeled off his T-shirt, stepped out of his flip-flops, and dived into the pool. He performed even, steady lengths, six strong strokes enough to propel him from one end of the pool to the other.

"I wish that was my husband," Lydia whispered to me, her eyes wistful.

I followed Vasili's progress up and down as if watching a slow-motion game of tennis.

"Do you know, it's just occurred to me that I've never seen my boyfriend swim. Which is odd because his twin brother's very keen on swimming." So was I. My mum, a swimming champion in her youth, had taken me to the pool since I was a toddler. While I was studying for my A Levels in Inverness, I worked as a lifeguard at the local public baths, saving up to travel in my gap year.

Lydia interrupted my thoughts. "Oh no, I don't mean I wish my husband was in that pool. I mean I wish my husband had a body like Vasili's."

I nearly choked on my glass of water.

Fortunately, the rest of our party soon joined us and we sat chatting until Stacey, last to arrive, tapped her pen against one of the water carafes to silence us.

"So, on behalf of *Writers' Weekly* Magazine, welcome to your writers' retreat on the idyllic island of Floros. I am sure that the staff of the lovely Hotel Ola Kala will make your stay a comfortable one, nurturing your inner writer with copious home-cooked food and plenty of the local wine to oil your creativity."

"She makes the local plonk sound like WD40," whispered Dominic.

"It tastes a bit like it too," said Tristram. "Especially the red."

Stacey pretended not to hear.

"So before we go any further, let's ask ourselves why we are here. What would have to happen, by the end of this week, to make you feel you've spent your time wisely?"

"And money," added Cecilia, avoiding Marina's indignant glare. "For those of us who've paid."

Stacey flashed an apologetic smile in my direction.

"I'm sorry, Sophie, I was forgetting. Let's all give Sophie a round of applause for winning her free place in our readers' competition."

Cecilia swivelled round to face me.

"What, you too, Sophie? You never said. So you're one more we're subsidising."

Ben raised a hand to silence her wrath.

"Come on, Cecilia, that's unfair. You won't be paying towards Sophie's trip. The magazine pays for that."

"Yes, it'll come out of its marketing budget for promoting the retreat," added Tristram. "I used to run a magazine once. I know about these things."

Stacey looked as relieved as I felt at their intervention.

"And this isn't the only retreat the magazine's running this summer. If you remember when you booked, there were eight dates to choose from. I've scheduled eight week-long retreats this season, and I assure you, none of the delegates have been subsidised by any one of the others."

Lydia raised her hand for attention. "I suppose you could say I've been subsidised as my husband paid." Then she shrugged. "But he only does it because he loves me."

"Just like my daddy," said Dominic, and the pair of them collapsed into giggles.

Stacey allowed their laughter to subside before continuing. "Now, let's try again. What would have to happen by the end of this week to make you feel the retreat had been a success?"

Lydia and Dominic stared at each other for a moment before falling about laughing again.

"Just don't tell my husband," said Lydia, slapping his bare knee. Dominic laid his hand over hers to keep it there.

Stacey coughed.

"Sorry, Stacey," said Lydia. "We'll behave now. I'm really trying, honestly. Shall I go first? By the end of the week, I'd like to be able to go home and tell my husband I've learned the basics of how to write a play and that I'm ready to have a go. Then he might let me go back to the drama group. Now you, Dominic."

"I need to convince my pa that I've done something constructive so he'll stop saying I'm a layabout."

Ben went next.

"I'd like to be able to decide whether it's worth trying to pursue my dream of becoming a writer of non-fiction books, researching deeply into topics that interest me, rather than forever scratching the surface for my paper. A week of focussed discussion will really help me. How about you, Dawn?"

"At present, as you know, I make money from multiple income streams, but I'd like to add another strand to my catalogue by branching out into historical novels. I'd like to plan the first one and write the first 20,000 words while I'm here."

"I thought you already wrote fiction, as well as your how-to books?" queried Stacey.

"Yes, but only in three genres so far. Then once I've mastered hist-fic, I plan to start a fantasy series."

I was feeling more inadequate by the minute.

"It's non-fiction all the way for me," said Tristram. "I want to make serious progress with my memoir of my career. It's taken me five years just to cover my early days before starting school, so I need to put a spurt on, otherwise I'll be dead before I'm forty."

Lydia looked puzzled. "Aren't you forty yet then?"

"I'm fifty-four in real life," he explained. "But if it's taken me five years to write up to my fifth birthday – well, you do the maths."

I wasn't sure she could.

Cecilia went next. "I'm refreshing my memory of the Ionian to write a serious literary novel set in Greece. I'd like to at least outline it so I can write it up when I get home."

"Kimberley?" Stacey ticked off her name on the list on her clipboard.

"I'm here for a career change. I'd like to launch a new career as a writer of romantic novels. I mean, I know all the theory. How hard can it be?"

Marina shook her head in disbelief.

They all turned to me as the only one left to declare their hand. I played for time.

"When I left home, my mother said to me, 'Just come back alive, Sophie.' Does that count?"

Everyone laughed politely, except Stacey.

"I think you're setting the bar a little low, dear."

I looked at the floor. "OK, well I'd like to make progress with my book project celebrating my late great aunt, May Sayers. You know, the famous travel writer?"

There were a few nods of recognition.

"I'm editing her letters for publication."

Marina uncrossed her legs and crossed them again the other way.

"Are you sure you're on the right course?"

I wasn't going to let her get away with such rudeness, no matter how many fans she had on social media.

"I'm writing the introduction," I said with all the dignity I could muster. "That's a big undertaking." But I couldn't keep up the façade. "Actually, I didn't mean to come on this retreat at all. My partner put me in for it without my knowledge. And now I feel a complete impostor. He should be here, not me. He's the real writer."

"Don't put yourself down, Sophie." I hadn't expected Cecilia to come to my rescue after her earlier outburst. "You're an independent, grown-up woman. If you want to write, go for it. Don't abdicate your ambition to your partner. If you don't root for yourself, then no-one will."

"But my partner –" I faltered. It was time to come clean. "Some of you might have heard of Hermione Minty?"

Even Marina had the grace to acknowledge Hector's pen name. It wasn't only in Wendlebury Barrow that his books sold well.

Ben quickly withdrew his arm from the back of my chair.

"Hermione Minty is your partner?" he asked. "I thought you said you had a boyfriend."

I realised with a start that I was on the brink of disclosing an important secret. I had to think fast to recover. Only Hector's mother, brother and I knew Hermione Minty's real identity.

"Well, he writes books a bit like hers."

Ben replaced his arm on my chair.

"You go, girl," said Cecilia. "Forget about that boyfriend of yours. Your project sounds important. May Sayers was a pioneer in her field. Let this week prove you're a writer. Just keep telling yourself how proud your aunt would be. And if it doesn't work out, hitch your wagon to a different star."

I was starting to warm towards Cecilia.

Dominic gave me a lop-sided grin.

"So, kill or cure then, eh, Soph?"

"Something like that, Dominic. Thanks, Cecilia. I'll give it a go." I looked about me for a moment, taking in the clear, bright pool water, the inviting array of sun loungers, the neat row of palms edging the garden and the old windmill on the hill above, its ragged outline clear against the cloudless azure sky. There were worse places to feel inadequate.

13 Signal Failure

Next Stacey tasked us with drawing up a one-page summary of the book we wanted to progress this week, and we spent the rest of the session making notes on a pre-printed template. Our homework for the next day was to write an elevator pitch summarising the unique qualities of our books and their commercial appeal.

"What's an escalator pitch?" asked Lydia.

Marina shook her head pityingly at Lydia's ignorance, but I was glad she had asked.

"It's a phrase borrowed from the Hollywood film industry," said Marina. "Suppose you're an aspiring screenwriter and you find yourself travelling in a lift – an elevator as they call them in the States – with a wealthy film producer. The elevator pitch is the short pithy description of your movie proposition that you might give him between floors to convince him to buy your script."

That made sense.

"How many floors?" asked Dominic, poker-faced, but with a twinkle in his eye.

Marina seemed unsure whether to take his question seriously. "Well, we're not talking Empire State Building."

"Thank you, Marina." Stacey took back control. "Now, off to lunch, folks. You've worked hard this morning. I'm aware I've been putting you all on the spot. It's emotionally draining to open up to strangers about your personal writing ambitions because they're so close to your heart."

"It's certainly an invasive process," said Kimberley. "I'm exhausted."

"Quite," said Stacey. "Which is why I recommend that after lunch, you take a siesta before you start on your homework. After your siesta, a little exercise would be good to stretch your body while your subconscious whirs away. A stroll by the beach, a dip in the pool – you choose. They eat supper late in Greece, not until at least 9pm. Any earlier and it's still too hot to enjoy a big meal, so you will have plenty of writing time between now and then to complete your assignment and fit in some writing of your own too."

As Stacey picked up her clipboard and bustled back into the hotel, the rest of us gathered up our notes, pens and other paraphernalia. Lydia scooped all her stuff into a capacious straw beach bag.

"So we've got all day to write something it would take us a moment to say in a lift? Sounds like we've got off lightly. Goody, I'll have time to do things I want to do."

Dominic, waiting for her, stood up and stretched.

Ben eyed them both analytically.

"Beware, Lydia. It takes longer to write the short version. I think it was Mark Twain who, when asked to make a public speech, replied, 'If you want me to speak for an hour, I'm ready now. If you want me to speak for ten minutes, I need a week's notice.' I know what I'm talking about, Lydia. Trust me, I'm a journalist."

"As did no-one, ever," said Tristram, unnecessarily rudely.

I leapt to Ben's defence.

"Hang on, Tristram, I thought you used to run a magazine? You must know tons of journalists."

"Exactly," said Tristram and, stripping off his T-shirt, he dived straight into the pool.

***

Though the pool looked tempting, my first thought after our excellent cold buffet lunch was to call Hector for help. Although he'd self-published all his novels, his long experience in the book trade meant he had a sixth sense for book marketing – what worked and what didn't. He'd be able to advise me on my elevator pitch, for sure.

After chatting with Ben for a bit by the pool and resisting his invitation to join him for a swim, I fetched my phone from my room, donned a sunhat and began the trek to Windmill Hill to get a signal. Halfway up, feeling a little dizzy, I realised I'd left my water bottle on my bedside table. Now I understood why Katerina had warned us to take our water bottles with us whenever we left the hotel. In this heat, even standing still, you perspired. On the move, without water, you'd dehydrate in no time.

I didn't want to waste time by going back for it. I wasn't planning to spend long up there. A quick chat with Hector, then back for that siesta, which, as my head grew muzzier, sounded increasingly appealing. I wished I'd put on some sun cream, too. Sitting in the shade of the pergola earlier, I hadn't realised how hot the sun was.

To my surprise, when I reached the plateau at the top of the path, Marina was already there. She must have had her phone with her all morning, planning to escape to the hill at the earliest opportunity. She was as inseparable from her phone as a teenager.

But she wasn't talking to anyone, just uploading photos and tapping in captions for her social media accounts. Perhaps she didn't have a partner or close friend to catch up with – only her fans to appease. I almost felt sorry for her.

"Ah, Sophie, just the person I needed!" Her aspartame smile made me wonder what I'd done to please her. Perhaps she'd found out that I worked in a bookshop, a fact I thought better to keep to myself in the present company. She held her phone out to me.

"Be a sweetie and take a few full-body snaps of me with the windmill, will you? Selfies are so limiting."

I obliged, following her instructions for multiple shots in different poses including wistful looks into the distance, notebook in her hand; leaning her back against the crumbling stonework, face turned to the sun; thoughtful shots, eyes half-closed, as if she were just writing a scene in her head. She didn't thank me when I returned the phone to her, just began scrolling through the shots, smiling or tutting in judgement, before uploading her favourites. Then, without even saying goodbye, she teetered back down the track. I hoped those wedge heels weren't the only shoes she'd brought with her.

Just when I thought I was alone, with the privacy I needed to speak to Hector, who should appear but Lydia? That surprised me. I'd assumed by now she'd be in the pool with Dominic – or sharing his siesta. Not far behind came Cecilia, striding along in khaki shorts, white vest and walking boots.

Much as I longed to hear Hector's voice, I decided now to text rather than phone. I didn't want anyone to know I needed help with my homework.

Cecilia, swinging a large water bottle, caught up with Lydia, who smiled sweetly at her.

"Hello, Cecilia. Have you come up to phone your other half too? Are you married or living with someone?"

Cecilia frowned. "Of course not. I'm here for me. This is a retreat. I don't want contact with the outside world. I've just come to admire the view."

I finished my text quickly and pressed "Send":

"Hector, help! I need an elevator pitch for May's collected letters. Go!"

I hoped he'd be as quick to reply.

To divert attention, I thought I'd better chat to the others.

"Hello, you two. It's a bit too hot up here for me. I'm not sure coming up here at midday was a good idea."

Lydia sighed and passed a hand across her glowing brow. "Me too, but I promised Bob I'd text him at every break in the schedule."

Cecilia took a swig from her water bottle.

"Really? That's such an imposition. It'll break the spell of the retreat for you to be thinking constantly about home. Why don't you text him to say the tutor said you're not allowed?"

Lydia's eyes widened.

"Oh, I couldn't possibly. I mean, he did pay for the course. It seems only fair."

"Do you think that gives him the right to dictate your behaviour?"

"It's not much to ask – only a text, not even a phone call."

Cecilia strolled over to the edge of the cliff, where she stood, arms wrapped across her chest, gazing out to sea. What was she thinking? For a moment her pose reminded me of Meryl Streep, waiting for her seafaring lover's return in the film *The French Lieutenant's Woman,* or Penelope watching for Odysseus's return. Either comparison would not have pleased her.

She turned round abruptly.

"And if he asked you to jump off this cliff, would you jump?"

I wondered whether Cecilia had ever been a schoolteacher. I edged closer to Lydia to present a united front.

"Maybe she misses him. There's nothing wrong with that. I've just texted my boyfriend, Hector, entirely of my own volition."

Cecilia drew back from the cliff edge and strode across to run her hand over the windmill's crumbling stonework. The door had long been boarded up, judging by the rusty nails and faded, splintery, greying wood.

"Oh, you two, you're as bad as each other. You are the puppets of men. You're too young to tie yourselves down. What are you, twenty-something?"

We both nodded meekly, as if our age was a weakness and our own fault.

Cecilia took another long drink from her water bottle, and I licked my lips. Lydia hadn't brought water with her either.

"Then live a little. Enjoy your freedom, your youth, your health, while you can. Look at those lovely boys by the pool earlier – Ben, Dominic and, er, Vasili."

"I did," said Lydia. You had to admire her candour.

"Play the field. Break a few hearts. Don't settle down yet. You'll only regret it later. If I were a little younger, I'd be in that pool with them right now. You're only here for a week. Lap it up while you can."

She turned to face the sea again, stretching out both arms to embrace the fine views. A generous scattering of boats, sails puffed out, were making the most of the afternoon breeze.

"Don't miss real life opportunities for the sake of your phones. Put them away till your return journey. Now is your time to be your true selves."

Was I not my true self with Hector? I began to wonder.

"So, if I take Dom, and Sophie hooks up with Ben, that leaves Tristram for you, Cecilia."

Lydia clapped her hands with pleasure. When Cecilia looked askance, Lydia shrugged. "Well, you are old enough to be the other boys' mother, aren't you? And you said to make the most of the opportunity to live a little."

Cecilia said no more, but strode back down the track, leaving Lydia and me gazing at each other like two naughty schoolgirls caught up to mischief. Then Lydia giggled and I breathed a sigh of relief.

"Oh well, let's get texting, shall we?" She grinned and set to work. She was still typing away when Hector's reply pinged into my inbox:

"*Fresh new insights into the private life of bestselling travel writer, the late May Sayers, from one who knew her best – her great-niece, author of a revealing foreword destined to delight Sayers's established fans and win a new generation of followers. Hxx*"

I might need a few floors in the elevator, but surely movie moguls were always heading to penthouse suites? It would have to do.

81

When I read it again, I realised how easily I could have come up with something like that on my own. Perhaps Cecilia was right. Maybe I didn't need Hector at all.

Anyway, now I could relax. A siesta in my shady, cool bedroom was calling. Just as soon as I'd absorbed a few litres of water.

14 In the Swim

Back in my shady pale-blue bedroom, Wendlebury Barrow seemed very distant, even unreal. Lying alone on the single bed, I felt liberated. Time to unleash my subconscious. I fell into a deep, dreamless and refreshing sleep.

On waking at around three o'clock, I drank the glass of water on my bedside table, refilled it from the carafe and downed a second glass. Then I slipped into my bikini, grabbed a towel from the bathroom, my sunglasses, hat and sun cream from the desk, and headed for the pool.

Dominic was rubbing sun cream into a prostrate Lydia's shoulders. From her sunbed, she raised her head slightly to smile in greeting, then lay back down, arms loose at her sides.

Dominic beamed at me as he screwed the cap on to the bottle of sunscreen.

"It's glorious down here. Where are all the others? They're fools to miss it."

Vasili emerged from the hotel lobby, bearing two tall iced coffees on a black plastic tray. As he set them down by Lydia's sunbed, he spotted my envious look.

"Shall I fetch another one for you, Sophie?"

"Thanks, Vasili, I'd love one."

I spread my towel on a sunbed, tactfully leaving an empty one between mine and Lydia's. I didn't want to play gooseberry.

When Lydia sat up to drink her coffee, she turned to talk to me across the gap.

"Where's Ben?"

"No idea. I've been asleep in my room since we got back from the hill."

"Shame. Remember what Cecilia said."

Dominic sat down beside her and continued massaging her slender back, all traces of sun cream long since absorbed.

"He's probably in his room writing his elevator pitch," I said, to remind them what they were meant to be doing. "Have you started yours yet?"

Dominic wrinkled his nose. "It's only one sentence. How long can it take? I'll do it later, before I go to bed." His hands stopped moving for a moment. "Or over breakfast. Depends whether I get any better offers in the meantime."

He pinged Lydia's bikini strap across her back.

"Yes, like Dom says, it's only a sentence, Sophie. How hard can it be?"

A voice came from above our heads. It was Ben, tapping away at his laptop on his balcony. He'd clearly been eavesdropping. I was glad I hadn't said anything more about him.

"I told you, it's harder than you think. You won't find some Greek muse whispering dictation to you on your pillow as you sleep."

Lydia shaded her eyes against the sunshine to see him more clearly. "No, but I might find an English one." She giggled, leaning against Dominic.

Ben just shook his head and continued typing. Embarrassed by their childish flirtation, I got up and lowered myself gently into the pool, the tepid water over my head silencing all sounds of typing and laughing.

Rising to the surface, I began a steady breaststroke. I concentrated on imagining Hector swimming beside me, wondering what style of swimsuit he preferred and what was his favourite stroke.

Soon I had fallen into a meditative state, the gentle lapping of the water against the side of the pool like a musical accompaniment to my progress, pounding a slow beat, up and down, up and down. I was glad no-one else had joined me, enjoying having the pool as my own private thinking space.

I had no idea how many lengths I had done when I finally allowed myself to flip over on to my back for a restful float. Drifting, weightless, I took a lungful of the warm herb-scented air and held it for as long as I could, spreading out my arms and legs like a starfish, closing my eyes to shut out the bright sun glaring down from the cloudless sky. Breathing slowly, I enjoyed the luxury of an empty pool where I didn't need to worry about bumping into anyone.

A loud splash, followed immediately by a shower of water droplets across my face, made me snap my eyes open. I swung my legs down under me and began to tread water as I looked to see who had joined me. Could it be Ben? For a moment, I couldn't tell. The diver remained completely submerged for a whole length of the pool. Then at the far end, up popped Tristram's salt-and-pepper curls, now slicked down to a silver wave. He began to churn up and down the pool, glancing occasionally at the chunky sports watch on his left wrist, apparently timing his progress. As a successful serial entrepreneur, he must have had a strong competitive streak, even when his only opponent was himself.

I glanced up at Ben's balcony expecting to see him still typing away. As someone who earned their living by their pen, he'd likely be the most disciplined and focussed of us all when it came to homework. If he wasn't working on his assignment, he might be progressing some journalistic project.

I was wrong. Ben had closed his laptop and was sitting back in his chair, staring at me since I didn't know when. The last thing I wanted to do was to lead him on. Hadn't he got the message by now? *Echo filo* replayed in my head like a mantra. I pretended I hadn't noticed his attention and turned to address Tristram, who had paused at the far end to catch his breath.

"Hi, Tristram, you can have the pool to yourself now. I'm going to my room to write."

As soon as I'd said it, I winced, hoping Ben wouldn't interpret that as an invitation to come knocking on my door.

Thanks to the heat, my costume was practically dry before I reached the top of the stairs. Changing into a vest top and shorts, I sat down at the desk in my room and pulled out the notebook I'd brought for the retreat and in which I'd been taking notes at the morning session. I copied Hector's text halfway down the next clean page before reverse engineering it into what looked like earlier versions of the polished final draft.

Was this really cheating? It wasn't like this was a school exam. Was I allowing myself to be over-dependent on Hector? If I'd been at home, I wouldn't have hesitated to ask his advice. The topic would have cropped up naturally in conversation and we'd have worked through it together that way. Talking things through was just another way of learning. What mattered was that I learned.

For a few moments I doodled around the finished elevator pitch, adding embellishments to the lettering, before laying down my pen. There, I was done, and there were still hours to kill before supper. What now?

I closed the notebook and lay it on top of the small pile of books on the corner of the desk: *The Odyssey*, my Greek phrasebook and my travel journal. Perhaps I'd read for a bit. All writers should read, I knew that much. My hand rested on the thick spine of *The Odyssey* for a moment, before of its own accord moving across to the travel journal. I'd been too tired to write in it the night before. I opened it at the still blank first page.

Dinah's kind smile as she'd presented me with the journal, memorable for its rarity, came back to me. She and the rest of my friends in the writers' group would be expecting me to fill these pages with my adventures, whether or not they ever wanted to read them. I couldn't let them down after they'd been so supportive. I should just start writing any old thing, and if I made a mistake, Jemima's unicorn would come to my rescue.

Extracting Auntie May's pencil from its box, I twisted the cap to expose a few millimetres of lead and stared at it for a moment. What words might lie locked within that little pewter streak? How often had my aunt thought the same?

I began to write.

***

A couple of hours and several twists of the pencil's cap later and I was still going strong. Not only had I summarised the journey and the morning's talk, I'd also written extensive character sketches of my retreat companions and hosts. This didn't feel like work at all. It was as easy as taking dictation. I was having fun.

Only when the open balcony door banged shut did I look up, half expecting to find someone out there. Of course, that was impossible. All our rooms were upstairs, and each room's balcony was completely enclosed by a waist-high wrought iron railing. It must have been the wind that had slammed my balcony door shut. Even so, I got up to check, opening the door and stepping out on to my balcony, its clay tiles baking hot beneath my feet.

Hot and surprisingly wet. Gone was the cloudless blue that I'd gazed at from the pool. Instead a seamless dark-grey blanket had covered the sky. Fat raindrops were pattering down. Below me the water in the pool jumped playfully as it received them.

A gust of wind chilled my warm limbs, rattling the sun umbrellas on the patio and rustling the vines wrapped around the pergola. All the other balconies, Lydia's to my right and the rest to my left, were empty of people, although most were bedecked with drying swimsuits and towels.

Dominic startled me by stepping out on to Lydia's balcony. He removed from the railing his surfer shorts and Lydia's bikini. Noticing me, he raised a hand in greeting, before casting his eyes skyward.

"That'll be the five o'clock blow that I told you about."

Lydia's giggled reply was muffled by the closed door, for which I was truly grateful. I retreated into my room and back to my desk to add to the character sketches that I'd started noting down in my travel journal. I needed to expand upon Dominic and Lydia's.

15 Ouzo's Revenge

Like cats made frisky by the wind, we were a lively group at supper. Vasili served us one dish after another, prepared by Katerina, who never left the kitchen for long.

"My mum says sorry about the sky," said Vasili above our chatter. He set before us a dish of aubergine fritters, still sizzling with droplets of hot olive oil and sparkling with great grains of sea salt. "We don't usually have clouds like this in May. Our rain falls in the winter. Summer storms are like hen's teeth here."

"Never mind." Dawn forked a couple of fritters on to her plate. "It'll focus our minds on our writing, which is what we're here for, after all. Besides, there are worse places to be confined to barracks. I for one am going to make the most of the writing time, free of any temptation to go outdoors until this storm's blown over."

Dominic took a slice of crusty white bread from the basket.

"Don't tell me you're still writing your elevator pitch?"

Dawn shook her head. "Done and dusted hours ago. I've finished outlining my historical novel, too. I reckon I can polish off at least the first couple of chapters before bed. Gotta get my daily words in, at least two thousand and preferably five. It's all about the words."

"I wish I could write that fast." Tristram's voice was mournful. "I'm struggling to reach my sixth birthday."

"Well, I'm not letting a passing shower put me off," said Lydia, glancing through the French windows that led from the dining room to a large balcony. "I'm going out of doors after supper. I've got to get up to the windmill to text Bob."

Dominic laid his arm along the back of her chair. "Do you want me to come with you? The wind will be stronger at the top of the hill. I could hold you down so you don't get blown away."

Lydia, eyes bright, laid a hand on his firm bicep. "You can be my ballast."

Marina laid down the fork with which she'd been picking at her plate of Greek salad and fluttered her eyelashes at him. "Will you hold me down too, Dominic? I must upload this afternoon's pictures."

I don't know who looked more alarmed, Lydia or Dominic.

"There's plenty of me to go around."

Lydia put her hand over her mouth to hide a giggle.

Marina turned to me. "How about you, Sophie? Have you got to report in to your romantic novelist friend?"

She enunciated the words "romantic novelist", applying air quotes as if I'd made a false claim on Hector's behalf.

"It's not a question of reporting in," I said tersely. "We just enjoy each other's conversation."

I was glad Hector wasn't there to hear me give such a dismissive summary of our relationship. I don't know why I was playing it down.

"Actually, I think I'll stay in my room and keep writing. I'm on a bit of a roll."

I didn't mention that my book plan was still untouched. But the travel journal was starting to fill up nicely.

***

The storm had raged into the night and was only just starting to abate as I headed downstairs for breakfast. All the other delegates except Lydia were there before me. Every time the door to the dining room opened, I looked up, expecting to see her coming to join the rest of us. The sound of flip-flops slapping on the marble tiles in reception raised my hopes, but it was only Katerina.

We'd just about cleared the array of bread, jam, honey, pastries, fruit and yoghurt when Lydia at last appeared, yawning, her hair uncharacteristically unkempt.

"Sorry, everyone, am I holding you up?"

"Don't worry, we've left some breakfast for you," said Dominic, although we hadn't particularly. It was all too delicious to resist.

Lydia pulled out the only empty chair, between Dawn and Cecilia, and slumped down into it, her eyes unnaturally wide, as if she was forcing them to remain open.

"I'm guessing it was that last ouzo that did it," she said, taking from the basket a piece of bread. She proceeded to pull it to pieces on her plate without taking a single bite.

Cecilia gave a wry smile. "Yes, it's always the last one, isn't it? Don't worry, we've all been there."

I was glad I'd taken Hector's advice to lay off the heady Greek spirit.

Lydia took more responsibility for her condition than I'd expected. "It's no-one's fault but my own." She avoided looking at Dominic, who was suddenly fascinated by the slices of melon on his plate. "You see, I never drink at home. I'm not really used to it."

"Who drinks ouzo at home anyway?" Cecilia's expression softened. "It's strictly a holiday indulgence. Eat that bread instead of playing with it, and have a spot of yoghurt if you can stomach it. Trust me, you'll feel better for it."

Stacey drained her coffee cup and looked at her watch. "And try not to be too long, please, Lydia. In ten minutes we'll be starting our next session." She dabbed her lips with her paper napkin and drew back her chair. "I think the wind has dropped enough to reconvene under the pergola at ten."

"Pergola at ten," repeated Lydia, staring at her crumbled heap of bread with as much enthusiasm as if it were human flesh.

***

"Next we're going to talk about the opening of your proposed book," said Stacey, after critiquing our elevator pitches. I was glad mine had gained her seal of approval, although to be fair we'd all got off quite lightly, even Lydia and Dominic. I was guessing she didn't want to discourage us before we'd really got going. "If it doesn't have a gripping opening chapter, whatever genre you write in, your reader won't get much further."

"That's one thing I have got sussed," said Tristram, leaning back in his wicker chair and clasping his hands behind his head. "I must have written the story of my birth at least fifty times."

"But is that the best place to begin?" Stacey leaned forward, her arms outstretched in appeal. "It may come first chronologically, but what has it got to do with your key messages?"

Tristram's face fell.

"You're targeting readers who want to learn to be entrepreneurs. The details of your mother's birth plan are hardly going to have them on the edge of their seats. Why not begin instead with your most remarkable business coup? Being born is a mere point of detail. It doesn't need to be spelled out."

"Yes, we've all been born, haven't we?" said Lydia, perking up. "Stacey's right, Tristram."

She was already starting to regain her usual English rose complexion.

"So what will your opening chapter be, clever clogs?" asked Tristram. He seemed unused to being upstaged by his juniors.

"Oh, Act I, obviously." Lydia stared away into the distance. "Plays always start with Act I."

Stacey brightened. "The three-act or five-act structure can apply to novels as well. Very good, Lydia."

I frowned. "That's a bit of a problem for me, Stacey, because all I'm writing in my book is my first chapter – the introduction to selected letters from my aunt."

Marina looked up from her phone. She'd been swiping through her picture gallery. "That's not writing, that's editing."

"Surely editing is a subset of writing?" asked Tristram, clearly still smarting from Stacey's earlier comment. "You can never have too much editing."

"Oh yes you can." Dawn tapped her notebook with her pencil for emphasis. "Sometimes good enough is good enough. Sometimes you just have to put the pen down, or you'll end up playing a game of writer's ping-pong with yourself – writing something, changing it, changing it back to the original, and going round in circles. If you want to write only one book in your life, carry on as you are. But I know what works for me. Knowing when to stop is a crucial key to productivity."

Marina nodded. "Know your reader and address their expectations."

"Which begs the next question," put in Stacey. "Who is your target reader?"

A few of us ventured a guess. I thought mine was easy. "My aunt's readers."

Stacey fixed me with an encouraging look, as if hoping to draw out a better answer. I was stumped. Dawn answered for me.

"Forgotten your elevator pitch already, Sophie? Also, readers who love travel writing who have not yet heard of your aunt. You can still grow her fan base even after she's gone."

Stacey sighed. "OK, I think we all need to clarify our thoughts on this point. Let's each spend ten minutes sketching our target audience, just as the fiction writers among you might prepare a character sketch. OK with that, everyone?"

She looked at each of us in turn for agreement, and we all nodded, except Tristram, who had tuned out and was staring into the distance at the windmill.

Lydia clapped her hands. "Ooh, lovely. That I can do."

16 Retail Therapy

After our buffet lunch, I decided to walk down to the harbour to think about my opening paragraph, which Stacey had set as our homework for the afternoon. If I hurried, I'd get there just as the day-rippers' boat was leaving. Watching the tourists might give me some good ideas on how to entice eager travellers to keep reading.

Still quite full from breakfast, I was one of the first to leave the lunch table. I set off at a quick march down the track that we'd come up on our arrival. I was glad of the persistent breeze coming off the sea to stop me overheating beneath the afternoon sun. At least the previous night's rain had made the air a little fresher. As I approached the harbour, I noticed the sea looked choppier than when we'd arrived, but there was something odd about it – something missing. There wasn't a yacht in sight. The harbourside was equally deserted, the jetty empty. I wondered whether the pleasure boat had sailed early.

I decided to stroll along the waterfront anyway. I hadn't yet met Katerina's mother. As she was the only other inhabitant of the island besides the monks, it would have been churlish to ignore her all week.

Ariadne was seated under the awning at the front of her shop, her wooden chair painted the colour of the sea. Her glum expression suggested that the day trippers had not arrived to avail themselves of her T-shirts, wind chimes, fridge magnets, shell necklaces and other cheap trinkets.

She brightened at the sight of me.

"Ah, young miss! *Ya sas*! *Parakalo*, you like to buy gift? Souvenir? T-shirt? Shoes?"

She pointed at an array of lavishly decorated plastic flip-flops in bright Ionian colours, suspended on hooks from the underside of the awning like so many pairs of overdressed kippers.

"Or nice scarf? You look very pretty in nice scarf. Blue, for you, I think, like your eyes."

She stood up to reach down a flimsy pale-blue cotton sarong, printed with the same dolphin pattern as Stacey's kaftan, edged by a Greek key pattern border. She pressed it into my hand.

I heard Hector's voice in my head.

"Puppy dog selling. Once a customer picks up a book and handles it, they're far more likely to buy. Who could resist the touch of a soft little puppy dog's fur? Who wouldn't want to take it home with them?"

I knew he used this technique to sell more books, but I didn't want a puppy dog, or a sarong, so hung it back on the rack from which she'd taken it.

"Thank you, it's very pretty, but not now. Maybe I'll come back another day. As I expect you must have guessed, I'm here all week at your daughter's hotel."

Ariadne slumped down on to her seat again. I could understand her disappointment. It was hard enough to keep Hector's bookshop in profit in a thriving village buzzing with visitors all year round. How tough she must have it here, with such a limited footfall and season. I don't suppose the monks were much help to her bottom line in winter.

"Where's the Lefkas boat today?" I indicated the empty harbour. "Shouldn't it be here by now?"

She shook her head mournfully then waved her hands at the jetty.

"It is the wind. No boats in this wind."

That explained the absence of pleasure craft.

I pointed at the sun. "But it's a beautiful day."

She shook her head again. "Too much wind. Too dangerous. No boats today. Tomorrow? I don't know. You buy postcard for your mother?"

Taking pity on her, I chose postcards for my parents, Hector, Joshua, Billy and Kate. Having persuaded me to buy stamps, she slipped the whole lot into a paper bag brightly decorated with the ubiquitous Greek key pattern. On a whim I added a fridge magnet for Hector with one of Homer's quotes, in what I took to be ancient Greek, modern Greek, English and French:

"Nothing is sweeter than home."

Her face lit up with a grateful smile as I handed over some euros, and it was only as I was about to leave that I realised I hadn't yet seen a postbox on Floros.

I turned and held the bag up to her and pulled out a card, miming posting it. "Where can I post them, please?"

She gave a broad smile. "On the mainland. Or give to ferry. When it comes."

***

As I headed around the rocky bay for a little while, the only further encounters I had were with a couple of lanky cats, long and thin as my Blossom would be if she'd been stretched out on a rack. I wondered whether they'd evolved this way to cope with the heat, needing more surface area for cooling down. With her jet-black fur, Blossom would have soaked up the sun like a sponge, poor thing. I hoped she and Joshua were taking good care of each other.

When I reached the end of the bay, the beaten earth track petered out, and I decided to turn back rather than continue across the rocks. I was wary of venturing further alone. If I slipped and sprained my ankle or broke my leg, no-one would know where to find me.

I hadn't realised quite how far I'd walked. When I turned round, Ariadne's shop looked like a doll's house in the distance. I was suddenly conscious of my isolation, as I had sometimes been in the Scottish Highlands, out walking with my father when I was younger. At least then I'd had him to protect me.

I quickened my pace, breathing a little faster and cursing myself for forgetting my water bottle again. Although the breeze was cooling, especially as my skin was veiled in perspiration, the sun was now in full force.

As I reached the shop's awning, Ariadne held out her arms to welcome me.

"Ah, you need drink after walk! I get you one. Or maybe ice cream?"

I closed my eyes in relief. "Oh, yes please! Both, *parakalo*."

"*Efharisto!*"

As she scurried inside to her fridge and freezer, I slumped down on to her blue wooden chair, which proved far more comfortable than it looked. I gazed across the water, rippling in the wind. Perhaps hers would not be such a bad job after all, sitting in the shade day in, day out, admiring this magnificent view: all those islands the tips of ancient volcanoes, mountainous beneath the waterline like sleeping monsters. Selfishly, I was glad the tourist boat hadn't come. This solitude was balm.

But so much for the solitude. Just then, a pale grey-haired man emerged from around the far corner of the building. As soon as he saw me, he turned on his heels and fled.

I wondered who he was and why he was so shy. Perhaps he was a monk on his day off? He wasn't wearing a habit, but the monks might not be the kind that were strict about clothing outside of the monastery's precincts. Perhaps they even went skinny-dipping on the monks-only beach, or donned Speedos. That might be why they kept the beach private, so as not to undermine their spiritual authority. I'd come across nuns who dressed normally when they went out to work in the community. This might be a plain-clothes monk. No wonder he fled at the sight of a young woman in minimal clothing. I was sure he didn't mean to be rude.

I hoped the monks brought Ariadne some business. Would God mind that much if they popped down here for the odd ice-cream? Especially when it was this hot. A little year-round custom from the monastery might make all the difference for her between solvency and bankruptcy outside of the tourist season.

All thoughts of monks went straight out of my head when Ariadne returned with a large cone of chocolate ice cream and a can of something fizzy labelled in Greek letters, a picture of a lemon on the side a helpful clue as to the contents. As I strolled back to the track, feeling restored, I saw Cecilia coming towards me. I waved my ice cream cone in greeting.

"Ariadne's ice-cream is well worth the walk." I paused to lick a melting chocolatey trickle. "And the view from the far end of the bay is amazing."

I pointed to the route I'd just taken.

"Thanks for the tip, Sophie, I think I will." She walked on.

Reluctant now to get back to work any sooner than I had to, instead of turning up the track to the hotel, I headed left on to the jetty. I slipped off my sandals and sat down, the weathered boards warm but rough beneath my bare thighs. As I dangled my feet in the crystalline water, shoals of tiny fish glistening like slivers of silver tickled my toes. My pulse slowed. This was bliss.

Having polished off the ice cream, I ground the remains of the cone between my palms and scattered them across the water, watching the fish dart to and fro to catch every last grain. The tiniest crumb must have been quite a mouthful for one of those little souls.

Back on my feet, I snapped back the ring-pull on my can of lemonade and sipped it slowly as I headed for the track. Cecilia, I noticed, had not progressed beyond the shop and was now sitting beside Ariadne, who had brought another blue chair out. Ariadne's conversation was much more animated than it had been with me. I guessed they were speaking in Greek. I hadn't realised Cecilia's Greek was so good, but then she had spent a lot of time in these islands over the years. I wondered what they might possibly have in common to talk about with such enthusiasm.

As I reached the path that led to Windmill Hill, I realised I'd come without my phone. I should have thought to phone Hector, having missed him the night before. I looked at my watch; I still had time to fetch it and phone Hector before supper. If I kept thinking about my opening paragraph on the way, it almost counted as work.

***

When I stepped out on to my balcony to fetch my towel from the railings, I was relieved to see Lydia sitting alone at the patio table on her balcony. To my surprise, she was busy painting a picture rather than doing her course homework.

"Lydia, you do realise that when Stacey said create a portrait of your target audience, she didn't mean do a painting?"

She grinned and looked up.

"Of course I do, Sophie. I'm not daft." She lay down her paintbrush and held up her work to show me. It was a skilful watercolour of the view down to the harbour. She'd captured not only the visual images, but also the sense of heat and the gentle breeze.

"Gosh, that's lovely. I wish I could paint like that."

"Would you like to see some more?"

Without waiting for my reply, she ducked into her room and returned with a slim black portfolio tied with a wide cerise ribbon. I reached across the gap between our balconies to take it from her, untied the ribbon and slipped the contents onto my patio table. There were four local landscapes, all taken from different angles from her balcony. Either she'd been spending less time with Dominic than I thought, or she was a fast worker in more ways than one.

I pulled out a picture of the windmill. She'd managed to capture both the weight of its weatherworn stonework and its poignant fragility. It made me realise how delicate was the balance of this island's microclimate: idyllic to tourists from northern Europe like us, but with the ever-present lurking danger of earthquakes and storms.

I held it up. "This one's my favourite."

She leaned across to look at it. "I've got a better one than that drying in my bedroom. I finished it just before I started the one I'm doing now. I'll show you when it's touch dry."

"Thanks, I'd like that. Anyway, I'm just off up the hill to phone Hector now. Do you want to come?"

She wrinkled her nose and picked up her brush again.

"Thanks for asking, Sophie, but I think I'll stay here and finish this picture. Then I'd better start on my homework. Although as I want to write plays, not books, it's not quite the same for me as for the rest of you."

I left her to it, hoping she wouldn't let herself be distracted by the sights and sounds of Tristram and Dominic in the pool below, racing each other up and down.

17 Over the Hill

The wind was picking up again as I strode out of the lobby and turned down the track. It wasn't yet time for the five o'clock blow, but already the gusts were enough to make the goats, so skinny compared to the plump Cotswold sheep I was used to, skitter about on the hillside, as if the breeze was chasing them. The storm had not done with us yet.

As I turned on to the path towards the windmill, a flutter of turquoise caught my eye: a sarong like the one Ariadne had shown me in the shop was caught on a thorny shrub. One of the other women in our group must have bought it and let it blow away in the wind. Surely not Cecilia? She was the only one I'd seen at the shop, but it didn't strike me as her style.

Would Stacey have bought it to match her kaftan? Unlikely. That would be a bit too much of a good thing.

Carefully, I disentangled it from the thorn bush and draped it about my neck like a scarf, planning to reunite it with whoever had bought it at supper. It was gossamer light. Worn as a shawl, it could easily slip off unnoticed, especially if the end got snagged on a thorn bush as you

103

marched past. It wouldn't be like dropping your car keys; it wouldn't crash to the ground.

I held up one end to admire it as I strolled on. Those dolphins were rather cute. Perhaps I'd go back to the shop the next day and buy one as a souvenir to remind myself of the pod we'd seen on the ferry from Sami.

As I climbed higher, I noticed significant damage from the stronger winds of the night before. Although it was still early in the summer season, and most of the vegetation was lush and green, some dry, leafless branches left over from last winter had snapped. Now they hung down from the trees like sinister hands waiting to grab me as I passed. I edged around them and was glad to reach the clearing on the plateau of the hill.

The wind was still strong enough to make the wooden framework that once held the windmill's sails creak and twitch. Before the earthquake, when the windmill was working and the canvas sails were still in place, it must have spun like a whirligig. My hair flew out behind me, away from my face as I looked out to sea. I felt like a human windsock.

Retrieving my phone from my handbag, I clicked on Hector's speed-dial icon, but couldn't get so much as a dialling tone. How close to the edge of the cliff dare I go to find a signal? Just how much did I want to talk to him?

Staring at the phone screen, I took a few baby steps forward, willing a bar or two to illuminate – enough to send a text, if not to host conversation. One, then two bars flickered on, so I quickly typed in an affectionate message, at the same time advising him that I might not be able to call or text till the weather settled. I pressed send and watched till the confirmation appeared, picturing the message being swept up by the wind and whisked across the sea.

Then I dialled my voicemail to retrieve two waiting messages – a jolly greeting from Kate that ended: "*No need to reply*" and the other from my mum telling me to mind the tides and the drinking water. Almost immediately a brief but welcome missive from Hector pinged on to the screen.

"*Hope you're having fun despite the weather. All quiet on the bookshop front. Too quiet. Looking forward to your return, Little Miss Noisy. Hxxoo.*"

As I was basking in Hector's electronic hugs, a shout from behind made me jump.

"Sophie, you didn't!"

"What?"

"Push Marina off the cliff!"

Ben pointed to the solitary turquoise flip-flop – another of Ariadne's wares – poised at the edge of the cliff. I'd been too busy trying to get a phone signal to notice it before. Then I realised there was another reason it was familiar: I'd seen Marina wearing a pair like it at breakfast. I'd been thinking it was only a matter of time before she fell off her wedges and twisted her ankle. How ironic if after swapping them for more island-friendly footwear, she'd tripped over her flip-flops.

Within moments of me dismissing his ridiculous accusation, Ben was scribbling in his reporter's notebook and snapping the evidence on his phone, declaring his intention to get a scoop on the story. He also sketched a map, showing the shape of the headland and the position of the windmill, flip-flops and phone.

He was acting too leisurely for my liking. "Don't you think we should be dashing back to the hotel to get Katerina to call the police?"

He shook his head. "No, far better to photograph the evidence first before it gets blown away. With this strong wind on such an exposed piece of ground, there'll be nothing to see by the time they get here."

He lay on his stomach, head and shoulders over the edge of the cliff, to photograph the second flip-flop on the ledge below.

"Please be careful, Ben!"

As I knelt beside his feet and gripped his ankles, worried he might slide forward, I tried hard to think of an innocent explanation for the whole scenario. Perhaps Marina had just been carrying the shoes back from the shop and dropped them without realising. That would also explain the lost sarong. Flip-flops are very lightweight, so it's not as though she'd hear them fall, especially against the sound of the wind. It would be a coincidence to drop her phone without noticing, too, but I've done that before with mine.

Ben crawled backwards, rose up on his hands and knees, then stood up and dusted himself down with one hand, raising his phone in the other.

"Can I take your picture, Sophie, as the one who discovered the crime? You could end up in my article, if the picture editor approves. I've got a disclosure form back in my room I'll need you to sign."

Before I could protest, he took me by the shoulders and positioned me to face the wind, my hair streaming out behind me.

"That's good. Now, one foot in front of the other, and clasp your hands behind your back."

I felt like Marina posing as a figurehead on Vasili's boat. I shuddered. Why was I letting him manhandle me like this? He could photograph me any time. There was no urgency. Perhaps it was the shock. Yes, I was paralysed by the shock of Marina's accident. I didn't want to believe his suggestion that she'd been murdered.

106

While he clicked away, I tried to talk without moving my mouth, like a ventriloquist, so as not to spoil the photos.

"You don't really think Marina could have been blown over the cliff, do you?"

"I'd prefer to think she'd been blown away rather than being pushed over, but I think that highly unlikely. Besides, there's no shortage of suspects to give her a shove, is there? She's put so many people's backs up, including yours."

I dropped my pose and swivelled round to confront him, hands on hips.

"What? How dare you! Just because we didn't –" I hadn't meant to speak about her in the past tense "– don't exactly get on doesn't mean a thing. If I pushed everyone who annoyed me off a cliff, I'd be a high body-count serial killer, and you'd be my next victim."

I snatched the sarong off my neck and thrust it at him.

"What are you trying to do, frame me? Getting me to incriminate myself by posing coldheartedly in a scarf Marina had just bought at the island shop? You'll be getting me to model the solitary flip-flop next."

Ben clutched at the scarf and looked at it, eyebrows raised quizzically. "This was hers, was it? So what were you doing with it?"

I clapped my hand over my eyes. Time to backtrack.

"I don't know. I saw one like it earlier in Katerina's mother's shop. They're the perfect colour match for the flip-flops she was wearing this morning, so she may have bought it at the same time. I just found it caught up on a branch on the way up here."

"Did you see her buy it?"

"No. I didn't even see her in the shop, only Cecilia."

"Cecilia fell out with Marina too, didn't she? Perhaps she pushed her over the cliff."

As I folded my arms, I felt chilly in the breeze without the sarong round my neck, so I slipped it back on. That might seem callous, but I'd only have had to carry it in my hands otherwise.

"Well, who didn't Marina upset? Besides, who's to say Marina didn't push Cecilia off the cliff? I saw Cecilia visit Ariadne's shop earlier. They're both forceful types."

He held up Marina's phone.

"Perhaps this will tell us."

I glanced at my watch before I spoke.

"For a definitive answer, we need to get back to the hotel and find out who's missing. Let's get Katerina to sound the fire alarm to get everyone assembled for a roll call. I think it's safe to assume that whoever doesn't turn up is the one who fell off the cliff."

"And if two don't turn up?"

"We'll have narrowed victim and murderer down to a choice of two. Then we just need to work out which is which."

18 No Smoke Without Fire

As we descended the track in silence, the wind remained strong. The creaking pine trees were on the wrong side of the track to offer us any shelter. We'd come down not a moment too soon. By the time we entered the hotel lobby, plump raindrops were spattering down on the marble patio slabs around the pool, like cynical angels spitting on our supposed island paradise. I was glad to get inside and close the doors behind us.

Katerina was at the reception desk, working on the hotel accounts. I was not looking forward to breaking the news to her. Not only was she a self-declared fan of Marina's books, she was also a hotelier whose business would suffer if her guests met fatal accidents – or worse.

Ben saved me the trouble. He leaned over the desk and reached for Katerina's hands. She didn't seem to mind.

"Listen, Katerina, we think something terrible may have happened. Sophie and I have just come back from the windmill where we found Marina's phone cracked and abandoned, as well as her new scarf and shoes. One shoe was at the edge of the cliff and one on the ledge below. I'm afraid it looks as if she's taken a tumble into the sea."

Katerina gasped and pulled her hands free from Ben's to put them over her mouth.

"You don't think she jumped? No, of course not. She was perfectly happy. She must have been pushed. Someone killed the famous novelist Marina Milanese at my hotel! Oh no, this is a disaster!"

More so for Marina than for you, I thought, startled by the shallowness of Katerina's affections for her favourite author. Then I remembered how Marina had offended Katerina on our arrival, in front of everyone else, refusing to sign her books. Katerina would be doubly regretful now. Marina's autograph would be worth even more after her death, the source cut off forever.

I laid a comforting hand on her arm.

"There's almost certainly a more innocent explanation. The sort that a court would rule death by misadventure. Perhaps she was blown over the edge."

Ben was quick to back me up.

"She might have simply not seen the edge while taking a selfie and taken a step back too far. It happens all the time at famous beauty spots around the world. My paper has reported such incidents before."

"I know for a fact that Marina was short-sighted, but too vain to wear her glasses," I added.

Katerina pulled a handkerchief from her apron pocket to wipe her eyes.

"She could not have been blown away by the wind," she said. "It was not strong enough."

"You're right, this is Floros, not Kansas," said Ben. "So I'm afraid she may have fallen against her will."

"But we don't know anything for sure yet," I said. "We didn't see it happen. Someone seems to have gone over the edge, considering there's a flip-flop halfway down the cliff, but it might not even have been Marina. She just seems the most likely, given the circumstantial evidence of her phone. We thought if you rang the fire bell, Katerina, you could assemble everyone and we can see who's missing. With any luck, she'll turn up. The dropped phone, shoes and sarong might all be red herrings."

I fixed Ben with a reproving look.

"Katerina, remember Ben is a reporter. He's just believing what he wants to believe to make a good story. No wonder he's jumping to conclusions. Honestly, Ben, this might all be a silly mistake."

Katerina shook her head gravely as she collected the fire drill folder from the shelf behind the desk.

"Oh, Sophie, I do hope you're right."

***

As the fire bell resonated across the bay, the three of us trooped out through the now steady rain to the emergency assembly point on the far side of the pool. Dawn, Stacey and Kimberley emerged from the bar, Vasili from the storage hut by the pool, and Tristram from the lobby, presumably having come down from his room. Vasili cupped his hands round his mouth and called up to balcony level.

"Guys, this is the real thing. Get down here to the checkpoint pronto, will you?"

The shutters of Lydia's room were flung open and Dominic stepped out on to the balcony.

Lydia's voice from within was petulant.

"I'm not going out in the rain."

But when Dominic saw us looking so serious, he headed back into the room, to emerge moments later from the lobby, his arm protectively around an anxious Lydia.

Katerina tapped her pen on her clipboard and sidled across to Vasili.

"Vasili, we miss Marina and Cecilia. Please check their rooms and turn off the alarm bell on your way."

Vasili nodded and broke into a run towards the entrance.

Lydia sighed.

"He's so brave!"

Dominic frowned.

"What do you mean?"

"Going back into a burning building to rescue Cecilia and Marina." She turned to Katerina. "I suppose the fire brigade will be here soon? I wonder what Greek firefighters' uniforms look like?"

"It is just drill, Lydia. Just drill. No worries."

Lydia pouted. "But you just said –"

Ben tutted. "Had to get you two lovebirds down here somehow. It was that or a bucket of water."

Vasili called down from Cecilia's balcony. "No sign of either of them in their rooms."

Perhaps Cecilia and Marina had wrestled on the clifftop, like Sherlock Holmes and Professor Moriarty at the Reichenbach Falls. Marina had angered Cecilia too, threatening to put her secrets in one of her novels on the ferry from Kefalonia. What awful secret was Cecilia hiding? Was it shameful enough to make her want to silence Marina?

Just then the distinctive sound of flip-flops approached up the dirt track. I held my breath while we waited to see who they belonged to. Cecilia, curly hair sagging beneath the weight of accumulated rainwater, stopped in her tracks, puzzled to see us all standing in the rain by the pool.

"Oh dear, where's the fire? I thought I heard an alarm down at the bay." She came over to join us. "Oh, hang on, don't tell me! Is this some kind of spontaneous team-building exercise?"

Ben didn't waste time answering her question.

"Have you seen Marina?"

Cecilia shook her head. "No, not since lunchtime. The only people I've seen this afternoon are Sophie by the jetty, an hour or so ago, and Ariadne. Ariadne and I had quite a long chat, actually."

"You've missed the fire," said Lydia. "But it wasn't a real one."

Tristram tapped his watch.

"What a waste of time. Why did you make us all come out here to stand in the rain, Katerina? I was on a roll just now, writing in my room. I'd reached the age of six." His chin jutted forward in defiance. "And by the way, Stacey, I've written a new opening – the party I held to celebrate making my first million. I still think readers will want to hear about my childhood, though."

Katerina lowered her eyes to her clipboard. "I'm sorry, Tristram, we needed to make sure you were all here."

We all looked at each other.

"But we're not all here," said Kimberley. "Marina's missing."

Ben laid a hand on Kimberley's shoulder.

"Yes, I'm afraid Marina is missing. Missing, presumed dead."

19 Dangerous Waters

Vasili set down two large carafes of red wine on the dinner table in front of us.

"No-one's ever fallen off that cliff and survived."

His face was glum. I wondered whether he'd lost friends that way. Perhaps tombstoning – jumping off cliffs for fun – was as fashionable among young people in Greece as it was in Cornwall. I hadn't seen any of those little roadside shrines on Floros, but then there weren't any roads.

Ben lay Marina's phone down on the table, gently so as not to damage the cracked screen further. I noticed he no longer seemed worried about fingerprints.

"The battery's run flat, so I've been unable to check it for evidence, such as incriminating photos of her assailant. Katerina's gone to get Marina's charger from her room and power it up."

Cecilia lifted one of the carafes and filled each of our glasses.

"Surely it's not for us to investigate, Ben? This is a job for the Greek police. We should leave it to them."

Vasili, returning with bowls of salted almonds, stood a little taller.

"Ah, that's my father you're talking about. He's the policeman in charge of Floros. He'll be here as soon as he can."

Tristram looked at his watch again.

"Surely he should be here by now? It's only a short hop from Ithaca, or is he waiting for you to pick him up in your boat?"

Vasili looked as surprised as if Tristram had suggested collecting him by flying saucer.

"In this wind? You're joking, mate. You don't want to add me to the body count, do you?" He nodded towards the open window. A cool breeze was wafting in.

"It's hardly gale force," retorted Tristram. "It's no distance. I reckon I could swim it in an emergency. And this is certainly an emergency."

"I wouldn't advise it," said Dominic. "Having sailed these waters so often with my dad, I know they're not as safe as they look. For all I know, the stretch between Ithaca and Floros could be as deadly as the one between Corfu and Albania. That channel looks innocuous, but beneath the picturesque photo opportunity lies danger. Dozens of Albanians have met their death trying to swim to a new life on Corfu."

Vasili frowned.

"It's for good reason that ferries don't sail in strong winds around here. Hidden rocks will hole a boat in moments if you get swept even slightly off course, and their shallow draught makes them vulnerable to capsize."

"What's wrong with a helicopter?" asked Tristram. "Doesn't your local police force have a helicopter?"

I guessed he was a frequent helicopter flyer. I pictured him landing on skyscraper rooftops for business meetings all over the world, wherever his latest deal took him.

Vasili raised his eyebrows.

"Listen, mate, in the current economic climate, we're lucky to have police at all. No worries, OK? I've phoned him already. He knows. My dad will be here as soon as conditions allow."

Kimberley rapped the table.

"And what are we supposed to do in the meantime?"

Vasili shrugged. "Do what you came for. You're only here for a week. Make the most of it. Life goes on."

"Not for Marina it doesn't," said Dawn. "And if, as Ben suggests, someone pushed her off the cliff, who's to say that person might not strike again? How can you honestly assure us that we're safe?"

Stacey scoffed. "What, you think there's a secret prowler here to bump off authors? A disgruntled reader who has taken against anyone who uses Oxford commas? Or a jealous aspiring author who resents our success and is seeking revenge?"

Dawn bit her lip. "If that's the case, that would explain why Marina went first. She sells most books. And I'd be next in line. I've heard of deranged authors seeking revenge on readers who left a vitriolic review. But I don't suppose Marina reviews other authors' books."

If she even reads them, I thought, but didn't say it aloud.

Lydia clasped Dominic's hand. "Well, we should be safe, Dom. We haven't written anything yet."

Kimberley set her empty glass on the table in front of her and stared down into it, as if hoping to find the truth in the residue, like reading tea leaves. Some of the dregs were as big as tea leaves.

"Who's to say her murderer isn't one of us? I mean, who else could it be, besides Ariadne or the monks? There's no-one else on the island. And each of us had good reason to be angry with her. The will to murder has to start somewhere."

"Well, who's to say it's not a mad monk, incensed by Marina's raunchier books?" said Dawn. "I've read her *Stallion Man* – strictly as research, you understand, for my billionaire romance series."

Cecilia tutted.

"What's wrong with that?" cried Dawn. "It's another income stream. Why shouldn't I? There are plenty of women prepared to pay good money for fantasies."

Dominic sniggered. Cecilia held up her hand to stop him.

"No stallion jokes, please."

"I used to love *Black Beauty*," Lydia sounded dreamy. "I read loads of horse books when I was little." I wondered whether she was writing any horses into her play.

Katerina returned with Marina's phone charger and an adapter to fit her British plug into a Greek socket.

"Dawn thinks the murderer might be one of the monks, Mama," said Vasili, stony-faced.

Katerina gasped and crossed herself three times before laying her hand on her heart.

"Please, no blasphemy. That will not help us."

"Or it might have been Yaya." (That's Greek for Grandma.)

"Do not be so foolish, Vasili. You know Yaya can no longer walk up the windmill track."

She collected Marina's phone from the table and plugged it into the nearest socket, leaving the phone on the windowsill. I sighed. By the time the police got here, there'd be no hope of finding useful fingerprints on it.

As a thunderclap reverberated above the hotel roof, Dawn reached for the second carafe of wine and refilled our glasses. Katerina picked up the empty carafe to return it to the kitchen.

"I better give you supper now. You must eat before you drink more. All wait here and I bring food soon."

20 Jumping to Conclusions

Having kept myself better hydrated that day, I suddenly realised that it had been a very long time since I'd been to the loo.

"I'm sorry, you'll have to excuse me a moment." I slid my chair back from the table. "Just popping out to the ladies'."

"I'll come with you," said Kimberley.

For a moment I thought she was suspicious of me and didn't want to let me out of her sight. Perhaps she thought I'd killed Marina and was now about to bump off Katerina. There must be lethal weapons in her kitchen, judging from how finely she sliced salad vegetables.

As Kimberley followed me into the toilets alongside the reception desk, I noticed her eyes were full of tears. When she'd closed the door behind us, I reached out to touch her arm.

"What's the matter, Kimberley? Do you know something? Do you know who did it?"

She stared at me for a moment, as if wondering whether to trust me. A tear trickled down her left cheek, and she brushed it away with the back of her hand.

"Not exactly. But the thing is, Sophie, I've been keeping something secret from you and from everyone here. I used to be an agent."

My mouth fell open. "You're a secret agent? Wow! Maybe we should put you in charge of the investigation until the police get here, instead of Ben."

Kimberley almost laughed.

"No, not a secret agent. A literary agent. I've been on the receiving end of manuscript submissions from more than one person on this retreat – including Marina."

She went over to the sink to splash cold water on her face. I sank down to sit on the floor, my back against the door to fend off unwanted visitors.

"But I thought Marina already had an agent? Some control freak who won't let her sign second-hand books? What bad advice. It was plain rude. I mean, how's the agent to know anyway if Marina just scrawled her signature across a few books on Floros? It would have meant so much to poor Katerina, especially now."

Kimberley ran her fingers through her damp hair.

"Yes, she's got an agent alright, but one who will only allow her to write the romantic drivel that she's famous for."

I frowned. Although I'd never read one, surely Marina's books couldn't be that bad?

"Aren't you being a little harsh? Her books might not be your cup of tea, but they sell in droves."

"Actually, even Marina thinks – thought – she was capable of writing something better. She was desperate to break into a different genre, something grittier and more challenging. And she was very good at the writing craft. She could write formulaic romantic novels standing on her head with her eyes closed."

Now there was a method I'd never tried.

"Her trouble was she was too good at it. Her publishers always want more of the same, because her readers do, and they are against her diversifying in case it loses them business. Marina did at least persuade her agent to submit her first psychological thriller manuscript to her usual publisher. But when they rejected it on the grounds that it was wrong for their target audience, the agent lost interest in it and tried to sweet-talk Marina into sticking with what she knew."

Suddenly I was seeing Marina in a fresh light. No wonder she came across as cynical. Perhaps she was being ironic rather than egotistical when she sneaked her books into the number one spot in the airport bookshop or sat reading one on the plane. She might have been crying inside.

"How do you know all this? Surely the conversations were private, between Marina, her agent and her publisher?"

Kimberley pulled a pocket-sized hairbrush from her handbag and turned to watch herself in the mirror as she ran it slowly through her hair, marshalling her curls into orderly waves.

"Because I'm the agent that she approached behind her current agent's back. About a year ago, after a few drinks at her publisher's summer party, we got chatting, and she confided in me about her frustration. I saw this as a great opportunity for the agency I work for and asked her to send my agency a submission with a synopsis and sample chapter. I hadn't really expected her to do so or even to remember our conversation. It seemed too good to be true. I was so excited when they landed on my desk by courier next day that I immediately asked for the whole manuscript."

She paused for a moment, fiddling with the bristles in her hairbrush.

"To be honest, it was stupid of me not to read her initial submission first. But I figured the worst thing that could happen would be that it didn't live up to my expectations, and I'd say no. Best case scenario: I could end up signing a big-name writer and instigating a multi-publisher auction, a multi-book deal, film rights, translation rights and more. Which would have meant megabucks for my agency, and a big bonus for me. Well, fifteen per cent of megabucks, anyway."

I was starting to see why Hector had sidestepped all the wheeler-dealing to publish his books himself.

"So how did that turn out?" I couldn't recall seeing any Marina Milanese thrillers at the airport, or at Hector's House, but the new book might still be in production.

Kimberleyslipped her hairbrush back into her handbag and pulled out her lipstick. She leaned forward to the mirror to scrutinise her mouth as she applied thick, even peach strokes.

"The manuscript was a dog's breakfast, Sophie. The plot was as holey as a cobweb, the characters defied belief, and she showed absolutely no grasp of international law essential to the story. I sent it back with constructive notes, inviting her to resubmit after implementing the changes, although I suspected it was beyond redemption."

She smacked her lips before blotting them with a tissue.

"I was right. When it came back, it was even worse. You can't polish a coconut. So I drew a line at that point and rejected it outright. There comes a point when you just have to say no and move on."

"How did she take the rejection?"

Kimberley pressed her gleaming lips together in a wide straight line.

"Not well. To continue the tropical fruit theme, she went bananas. She sent me a series of emails fuming about how her readers knew better than I did, how millions of satisfied customers couldn't be wrong. She copied them all to my boss. She was after my blood."

She crumpled the tissue and dropped it in the wicker wastebasket.

"Of course, I took no notice. I knew I'd made the right decision, and my boss stood by me. But, oh, Sophie, the desperation in those emails! I quickly turned from being irritated by her arrogance to being moved by her dilemma. But I was powerless to help. I was just doing my job."

"But how did you feel when you realised she was the guest novelist on this course? Surely you feared that would create an awkward situation, to say the least?"

"Not at all. You see, our correspondence was online. We never met or spoke in person."

"But your name? Kimberley is pretty unusual. Surely she'd remember your name."

Kimberley looked a little more cheerful.

"Oh no. You see, she never knew my real name. At the agency, when we're reviewing submissions, we operate under aliases. The agent was Pamela Jones, as far as she was concerned. It's company policy to protect its staff from authors angry at our rejections. I believe they do the same with the civil servants who respond to letters sent to the Prime Minister. It's to fend off mad stalkers with weird political agendas who might follow them home or trash them on social media or worse. Besides, if circumstances change, we might want to take rejected authors on another time – under a different alias, of course."

I got up from the floor to run some water into the sink and splash a little over my face and neck. This tiny windowless room was getting hot and stuffy.

"So why worry? It's not as if she found out who you were, and it's too late for her to seek revenge on you now."

Kimberley chewed her lip, regardless of her newly-applied lipstick.

"Because you see, Sophie, her letters were so distraught that I thought perhaps I'd pushed her too far. You've seen what she's like in person – full of self-important bluster. Now I realise that underneath she's very vulnerable – fragile, even. I kept telling myself that as a professional fiction writer, she must have a thicker skin than this, and perhaps her hysterical emails meant no more than the tears of a seasoned actress. But her words stayed with me."

I didn't know which of them to pity more.

"When the emails stopped coming, I wondered whether it had all got too much for her. Honestly, Sophie, I know people can be a bit rude about agents, and they think we're all heartless – at least those authors who never get signed – but having to reject a manuscript that clearly meant so much to her was really hard. That's what made me decide on a career change, and to come on this retreat. I'm planning to resign from the agency when I get back. I want to write novels myself. I've always been the bridesmaid, never the bride. Now it's my turn to shine. While I'm establishing myself as a novelist, I can freelance as an editor and proofreader. That's how I got into publishing in the first place. Then on the side I'll write novels. I know all the tricks, and I have all the right contacts to make a go of it, I really do."

"So why go to the expense of coming on this retreat?"

"The usual reasons – to surround myself with writers, get myself motivated, and I love the Greek islands. And then when I discovered Marina was here too, I was delighted. Coming here had given me the unexpected opportunity to become a personal friend of hers. I thought we might help each other. I'd help her transition to a different genre, and she might help me launch my career."

I wrinkled my nose.

"That didn't really work out, did it? I'm sorry about that. Do you think it's because she recognised you from her publisher's party, when you first approached her?"

Kimberley shook her head.

"I'm pretty sure she didn't. I've changed my hair colour and style since then, and lost a bit of weight, so I look quite different. Plus of course the name of the villain that stuck in her mind was Pamela Jones, not Kimberley Houston. Even so, once I'd met her again over here, I found her too scary to even broach the subject. I'm still scared now – because, don't you see, Sophie? I don't think she's been murdered at all. I think she's killed herself. I think my ruthless, heartless rejection of her in the face of all her pleading might have been enough to push her to suicide. She'd given up hope."

I helped myself to a squirt of olive oil hand cream from the tube by the washbasin, massaging it slowly into each finger joint.

"If it makes you feel any better, I suspect she may still have the last laugh."

Kimberley stared at me in disbelief. "What, from beyond the grave?"

I nodded. "You see, Kimberley, I've been keeping a secret too. My day job is a bookseller, and I know about these things. I don't suppose there's any chance you still have that rejected manuscript, is there?"

She shook her head. "No. If we kept all the rejects on file, our computers would seize up. We delete rejected manuscripts as a matter of course."

"Shame. Because if Marina really is dead, her first and last psychological thriller, no matter how ropey, could have netted you a fortune."

"Aargh!" Kimberley enmeshed her fingers in her curls, undoing the good work of her hairbrush. "When my boss finds out Marina's dead, he'll go mad. I'll go down in publishing history on a par with those agents who rejected J K Rowling. I'll never work in publishing again."

21 A Late-Night Visitor

Over supper, it became clear that Kimberley wasn't the only one in our party fearing for her career. With seven more retreats to run before the end of the summer, Stacey was keen to continue with our agenda, with or without Marina.

"After all, there's nothing we can do until the police get here. And you've all paid to be here."

"Or most of us have," murmured Cecilia.

Ben smirked. "Next you'll be telling us it's what Marina would have wanted."

Dawn came to Stacey's defence. "If it was me in Marina's unfortunate position, I wouldn't want the rest of you to be thwarted by my death."

Tristram drummed his fingers on the table.

"If you stop now, you'd be obliged to offer us either a refund or a place on a future retreat. And I for one don't have a window in my schedule to return in the foreseeable. I vote we carry on."

Ben glanced at Vasili, who was busy clearing empty plates from our main course. It said a lot for Katerina's cooking that not a scrap of pastitsio remained, despite our collective anxiety.

"That would be best for your mother too?"

"Sure, mate," said Vasili. "If you all slink off home now – not that you could, as we can't leave the island till the wind blows itself out – she'd be well short of cash on the bar takings. That's enough to make or break the business these days. And as for refunds –"

"I don't know how you stay afloat with such a limited season and access," said Tristram.

Vasili shrugged. "Every little helps."

"Anyone disagree?" Stacey looked around the table for a show of hands. No-one raised theirs.

"Even without Kimberley here to vote – where is she, by the way? – the decision's clear."

"She's gone to her room to lie down," I said. "She's fine but doesn't want to be disturbed."

"I suppose the show must go on," piped up Lydia. "But will we be able to concentrate with a murderer on the loose?"

"On the loose?" said Dawn. "Really? My money's on it being one of us. To my mind, the police can't get here soon enough."

***

"Psst! Sophie!"

I was just about to enter my room for the night when I heard Ben hissing to me from further down the corridor.

"What do you want?" I hissed back, hoping no-one else would emerge from their room and get the wrong idea about me and Ben. He tiptoed down to my door.

"What was all that about between you and Kimberley earlier? You were about half an hour in the toilets together. Did she tell you anything interesting? Any clues

130

to share? Don't tell me you extracted a confession from her and have her handcuffed in her room, awaiting the arrival of the police to make it official?"

"Sure, I never travel without a pair of handcuffs. Do you? Honestly, Ben, your imagination really is working overtime. I reckon you should ditch your non-fiction ambitions and start writing fiction."

He grinned. "So, you don't think Kimberley's implicated?"

I shook my head. "Of course not."

"So who?"

Against my better judgement, I beckoned him inside my room, nervous of discussing the matter in the corridor where anyone might hear us. Also, I had a feeling there was something he wasn't telling me. He might be more likely to reveal it in the privacy of my room.

"Then who else?" he persisted.

"Not Stacey, for a start. Nor Katerina, nor Vasili. Their livelihoods depend on the retreat's success. They're hardly going to bump off delegates."

"How about Dominic or Lydia? They could have ganged up on her. And I wouldn't want to pick a fight with Tristram. He's got such a sense of entitlement that he'd defend his ego to the death. His and Marina's would be quite a match."

"What about Cecilia? Do you think Marina was blackmailing her? She seemed very upset when Marina threatened to turn her secrets into a story."

"Did she? When? I didn't hear that."

"I forgot you weren't there. It was when we were travelling from the airport together. Just Cecilia, Marina, Lydia and me, before we'd met you. But it's still a bit thin."

"Sounds like the most likely motive for murder so far. I could understand if any of us had just slapped her, but murder? Quite the overreaction."

He put his hands on my shoulders.

"You'd better look out, Sophie. Perhaps if it is a blackmail thing with Cecilia, and you and Lydia are the only other witnesses to her argument with Marina, the next victim will be one of you." He looked about the room for a minute. "Dominic will keep an eye out for Lydia, I'm sure, but do you want me to stay here tonight to keep you safe? I don't mind."

When I pulled away from him, he dropped his arms to his sides and slipped his hands innocently into his pockets, accepting my rejection with good grace. Then I grabbed his shoulders, spun him around and marched him back towards the door. I thought it best to make a joke of it.

"No, thank you very much. I don't want to find our night of passion splashed across the pages of your paper when we get home. *Echo filo*! I have a boyfriend."

As he opened the door, the cheeky smile of one whose dishonourable intentions have been rumbled played about his lips.

"Besides which, for all I know, Ben, Marina's murderer might have been you."

We locked eyes for a moment, before I closed the door behind him and locked and bolted it.

Only then did my heart begin to pound. Was that really such a joke? For all I knew, Ben could have been the murderer. Hadn't he been first on the scene after me? He could easily have heard me coming and hidden behind the windmill or in the undergrowth until I arrived to make it look as if I was first on the scene, the murderer discovered.

132

To be on the safe side, I bolted the French doors to my balcony and settled down to a hot, sticky, airless night.

22 The Search Party

Next morning we needed jackets and sweaters. The breeze had not dropped all night. At home in the Cotswolds I'd have called these weather conditions fresh, rising to bracing, but after the glorious warm sunshine that had welcomed us to Floros, we felt positively chilly.

Over breakfast, Katerina told us that she'd already spoken to her husband for an update on his expected time of arrival, and the news was bad. The wind was still too strong for a water-taxi from Ithaca and, looking at the forecast, he didn't expect to arrive for another twenty-four hours, when more seasonal weather was due to return.

"I am so sorry about the weather," she said, circling the table to top up our cups from the coffee pot.

"The weather's less of an issue than the death of one of our party," returned Cecilia, slicing bread from the big white loaf with a huge saw-toothed knife. "But having slept on it, I'm not convinced it's murder. How do we know Marina hasn't just passed out somewhere from dehydration? You've been warning us about that since we arrived. Or fallen down a ditch and got stuck, twisting her ankle on those ridiculous wedges. Or she might have holed up somewhere to shelter from the rain and forgotten her way back to the hotel."

"Or she might secretly be a man and have gone to join the monastery," said Dawn brightly. No wonder she was able to churn out so many novels when her imagination teemed with ideas.

Kimberley, puffy-eyed, looked up from her scrambled eggs.

"Or she might have taken cover in somebody's woodshed and accidentally got locked in?"

I was pleased to hear hope in her voice.

Tristram raised his eyebrows. "What, like a stray cat?"

"There are plenty of abandoned buildings left over from the earthquake," I observed.

"Well, that fits," said Cecilia. "She'd be the sort to head straight for cover at the first drop of rain to save spoiling her hair."

Lydia set down her butter knife. "Really, Cecilia, there's no need to be so unkind. I believe she's tougher than you think." I suspected Lydia might be too, for all her fluffy exterior. "Honestly, I'd rather be stuck in a lift with Marina than with you, for all your feminist principles."

Dominic patted her thigh approvingly.

"Me too. Marina would be more likely than Cecilia to have a hairpin or nail file about her to fix the lift mechanism."

"Ooh, that reminds me," said Stacey, raising a forefinger. "In your free time today, please practise your elevator pitches to each other to your heart's content and see whether you can improve upon them. Anyway, back to the point: we may not be able to do much to help her if she has fallen from the cliff, but the least we can do is search any outbuildings or abandoned earthquake ruins.

How foolish would we feel – and how angry would she be – if she'd been shivering all night, stuck in some earthquake ruin while we slept in our cosy beds as if we hadn't noticed she was missing?"

"I wouldn't put it past her to stage her own disappearance, like Agatha Christie all those years ago," said Cecilia. "It certainly boosted *her* book sales."

I frowned. "There's a compelling theory that Agatha Christie's disappearance was the result of stress-induced amnesia, caused by her husband telling her their marriage was over."

Ben was scribbling fast in his notebook. "I wouldn't mind a scoop on that."

Kimberley got us back on track.

"Anyway, what happened about Marina's phone? You recharged it last night, Katerina. Has anyone checked it out yet?"

After setting a bowl of fresh strawberries on the table, Vasili raised his hand.

"Sure, mate. I tried it late last night, but I couldn't get beyond the phone's security. It needs her fingerprint. Given enough time I might guess a numeric password, but I can't fake a fingerprint for love nor money."

There was a silence while we absorbed this disappointing news. Then I had an idea so obvious I wondered why no-one had suggested it before.

"What are we thinking? We don't need to crack her code. Of all of us, isn't Marina the most likely to have shared something on social media while she was last on the hill? She has been posting since we arrived – she lives her life online. Every little experience ends up on her fan page."

"You mean you follow her on Facebook?" Ben looked amused and I blushed.

"I just started following her on Saturday after I sat next to her on the plane. I wanted to see whether she was always like that."

Katerina, pulling up a chair to join us, narrowed her eyes.

"Like what, exactly?"

I chose my words carefully.

"Confident. Outgoing. Expressive about herself and her work. Assertive."

Ben let out a bark of laughter. "An egotistical cow, you mean."

I gave him a reproachful look. "For someone who is after a scoop on her, you should show more respect."

"Oh, as if she's likely to turn down the chance of a feature in a national daily if I don't exactly kowtow to her. I don't think so."

Kimberley intervened. "You'll need the agreement of her agent too, don't forget."

Ben went quiet and toyed with his pen.

"Surely you have internet access on the hotel computer, Katerina?" asked Tristram. "How else do you fill your hotel without a website or social media presence?"

Katerina looked obstinate. "I manage. I have not many rooms. One phone call from Stacey Sydney and I am eight weeks full."

"Then we'd better go up to the windmill to get a signal and check out her final Facebook posts."

"I'll go." Vasili got up and headed for the door. "I'll save any posts to my phone so you can all see them when I get back, even offline."

Katerina nodded approval to her son, and he left without more ado.

"But Stacey's right," Kimberley continued. "I say we ditch this morning's session – or postpone it, at least – till we've formed a search party and inspected all possible places of shelter. Katerina, can you tell us where we ought to look?"

"I get map."

Katerina fetched some photocopies of a footpath map of the island. There were very few routes as the island was so small.

"The old village destroyed by the earthquake was only along the bay – about a dozen houses. The islanders were mostly fishermen. The land here cannot be farmed. There was goatherd too." She ran her finger along the outline of the bay. "My mother's shop is first of houses. She show you this morning."

"What about her shop?" As a retail worker myself, I knew how important it was not to close without warning. A shop must keep regular opening hours.

Katerina waved my objection aside. "No tourist boat will come today. You are her only customers."

"And the monks," I added, but she shook her head vigorously.

"The monks grow own food," she said. "They never leave monastery except to swim in sea."

Dominic grinned. "Maybe Marina went to chat up the monks."

Cecilia laughed. "Essential research for her next book, do you think? *Monks in Love*?"

"That title alone could be enough to make the monks push her off the cliff," said Dominic.

When Katerina crossed herself, I realised we were once again veering on the blasphemous.

"I'm sorry, Katerina. Everyone's getting a bit silly now. Let's get on with the search. Where else should we look? Is there any chance she could have taken cover in the windmill itself?"

"If she did," replied Ben, "she also managed to nail planks of wood over the door on the outside after she'd done so."

I'd forgotten the door was boarded up. Presumably the inside was too dangerous to enter after the earthquake.

"There's only one footpath across the top of island," said Katerina. "The main footpath leads to the monastery. It is a long way and a hard climb."

"Lydia, how about we cover that route?" said Dom. "We're young and fit."

"I should say so," said Lydia, winking at Dominic.

"Ben and I had better not do the windmill again," I said. "Better to have fresh eyes on it. Katerina, do you want to take a couple of people up the hill? Ben and I can do the bay."

"I will take the windmill," agreed Katerina. "Dawn, Kimberley, Tristram, you come with me."

Cecilia raised her hand. "I'd like to go to the bay with you and Ben, Sophie, and then I can translate for Ariadne."

So Cecilia was as good at speaking Greek as I'd thought. I wondered why she'd kept it to herself. If I'd been that fluent, I'd have been chatting to Katerina and Vasili in their native tongue, or at least saying more than the *parakalo* and *efharisto* that I'd mastered so far.

"That leaves me for the bay as well," said Stacey. "It's quite a big area. Shall we split up?"

"You and I go left, Ben and Sophie go right," suggested Cecilia. "There are some shallow caves on the right-hand side, so make sure you check in those, Sophie."

"Maybe Marina got cut off by the tide in one of the caves," said Lydia.

"The Ionian's not tidal," chorused Ben, Dominic and I.

"But she might have taken shelter from the storm in there," I considered. "And then had a heart attack or something."

"Marina didn't strike me as the sort who'd be frightened of a thunderstorm," said Tristram. "Not enough to give her a heart attack, anyway."

Stacey put her hand over her chest, fingers spread wide.

"Congestive heart problems can be asymptomatic, especially in ladies of a certain age."

"People of a certain age," corrected Cecilia.

Tristram pushed back his chair and rose from the table.

"Either way, I don't think we should waste any more time. I can't believe we didn't search for her yesterday. Let's not wait for Vasili to return, we'd better set off right away."

In hindsight, I too was horrified at our delay. But Ben, focussed on his ideal newspaper story, had seemed so single-minded about it being a murder, he'd almost convinced us that was the only option. Wishful thinking on his part? "*Famous author accidentally locked in shed*" would certainly not sell as many copies as "*Romantic novelist in clifftop death plunge horror*".

"We'll reconvene the course after lunch," said Stacey as we headed out of the hotel lobby to disperse in different directions. "That is, unless there are any developments with Marina that need to take priority."

"And tomorrow the police will be here," added Katerina. "Then they can take charge."

23 On the Trail

As it happened, Vasili was returning from the windmill as we left the hotel. The evidence from Facebook was pretty conclusive. Amidst the barrage of selfies, showing Marina smiling coyly with various scenic backdrops, were a couple of Facebook live videos.

Her latest video began with her back to the cliff edge. The camera faced away from the windmill as she effused about the colours and clarity of the sea behind her, then panned the thick pines on the far side of the track that led up to the plateau. There in the distance, amongst the greens, browns and greys of the undergrowth, fluttered a streak of cobalt blue like a sail. Although at this distance the dolphin pattern was indistinguishable, it was undoubtedly the sarong that I'd extracted from the bushes on my way up.

"Oh my days!" Marina commentated. "That flash of blue is my new sarong, which I bought this afternoon from the most delightful little Greek gift shop on the bay. Now, wouldn't that make a gorgeous book title? *The Little Greek Gift Shop on the Bay*. I may just have to write it on my return. But please don't worry, I'll collect the sarong on my way down. I may even offer it as a prize to members of my readers' club to mark the publication of that book. Would you like to win it? Visit my website now to join my mailing list and be entered for all my free draws."

My goodness, she was a one-woman publicity machine, even in death. I remembered how cosy the sarong had felt when I'd looped it round my neck. Perhaps it was still warm from her body heat. I shuddered.

Then Marina turned her phone camera slowly to her left, eventually alighting on the derelict windmill.

"The Little Greek Windmill on the Cliff. That should be the sequel? Do leave a comment – I'd love to know what you think."

The windmill was creaking and twitching, as if in protest.

She continued to pan left, across the wild rosemary bushes, and the picture jumped slightly as a pair of goats emerged and trotted across in front of her, heading for the track. No need to arrest any goats, then. They were on their way downhill as Marina made her final address.

"And now for the grand finale – the stunning view from the clifftop across the sea."

The 360-degree tour complete, the first video ended. Then came a second, showing Marina with her back to the cliff edge, stepping slowly backwards, talking all the while about the magnificence of the local colours – the greens, the blues, the whites, but using the vocabulary of a watercolour palette to describe them. She seemed surprisingly distant from the camera. I hadn't realised she had a selfie stick, but that didn't surprise me.

Suddenly the image blurred, before resolving in a close-up of earth and pebbles. The only soundtrack now was the faint bleating of goats, the now familiar jangle of their neck bells, and the breeze passing across the grass. After a few minutes of inaction, the film ended, presumably shutting off automatically when the camera detected no further significant sound or movement. The timestamp of the start of the recording was about twenty minutes before I'd arrived at the windmill. By the time we found the phone, Marina could have been far away, bobbing on Ionian waves – or under them.

Ben thumped the lobby table with his fist. "Oh no, that's my scoop scuppered."

Vasili shook his head. "Don't worry, Ben, judging from the comments her readers have left, they think this is either a technical hitch or a joke. They're saying things like: 'Not another cliffhanger ending!' and 'That's it, Marina, always leave us wanting more!' and 'Enjoy the rest of your holiday'."

"But what about her family? People who know her in real life?" I imagined what my parents would think if they saw I'd posted something like that. "If I was her mother, I'd be out here on the next plane to look for her, hoping to find her still alive. She might just have tripped over and fallen forward, rather than backward, knocked herself out for a bit, and then got up suffering from concussion. The ground is very hard up there. She might have been so dazed that she forgot to pick her phone up."

Vasili lay the phone down respectfully and we all fell silent for a minute or two. Dawn was first to speak.

"You're right, Sophie. We'd better go out and search without delay."

Tristram looked away for a moment. "Yes, we should. If we don't, won't the police, when they finally arrive, think it odd that we haven't done so?" He gazed at us each in turn. "And that might make them think that at least one of us has something to hide."

***

Ben and I parted company from Cecilia and Stacey at the jetty and headed right. I'd not been as far in this direction on my previous stroll. Whereas I'd enjoyed the solitude then, in the current circumstances I was glad of Ben's company.

The footpath ended a few hundred metres beyond the jetty. We stepped down on to the narrow shingle, barely wide enough to accommodate the two of us walking side by side. The shingle continued for only a few hundred metres more before tapering to a point at the foot of the cliff, which jutted a long way out into the water, screening the coast beyond.

We hugged the edge of the strand, following the line of shallow caves to inspect every nook and cranny. To my relief these were well lit by the midday sun and held no sinister dark alcoves to harbour bats – or, indeed, romantic novelists. I'd been hoping Marina might leap out on us, like in a childhood game of hide and seek, just as little Jemima had suggested when she gave me her unicorn eraser in the bookshop before I set off for Greece. But no such luck.

I stooped to pick up a smooth pebble of sea glass, glinting in the brightening sun, and slipped it in my pocket. I can never resist sea glass, always wondering about its origins and its backstory. I had a jar full I'd collected from Scottish beaches at home.

When we reached the end of the shingle, Ben slipped off his sandals and held out his hand to me.

"Come on, Sophie, let's wade out as far as we can. The water's really shallow here."

He took a few steps into the water, ankle deep.

"Ooh, that feels good. Don't worry, it's really clear. You're not going to tread on a jellyfish."

He took another couple of steps and turned to check the progress of the search party on the far side of the bay. With the aid of a stout stick, Ariadne was hobbling beside Cecilia, while Stacey strode purposefully ahead.

"Come on, Sophie, come and join me. We'll still be back way before the others."

I didn't like to say that I was worried that if we waded out, Marina's bloated body might float by us. So I stepped out of my own sandals and waded out to join him.

The water was indeed delightful. The pebbles, churned over and over by the sea for thousands of years, were tiny enough to provide a gentle foot massage. I refused Ben's hand until I twisted my foot in an unexpected hole. Instinctively I grabbed him to steady myself.

"Safety in numbers, eh, Soph?"

He squeezed my hand for reassurance, then remained gripping it too firmly for me to let go.

We waded on till the water was up to the bottom of my shorts. I glanced across to Cecilia's party, wishing they'd turn back and see where we were. I felt awfully vulnerable.

"I – I don't think I want to go any further out."

Ben stopped and turned round, swapping hands before I could stop him. My freed right hand ached from his strong grip. Now it was my left hand's turn to suffer.

I focused on the clifftop ahead of us. Now we were this far out, we could see the windmill, side on.

"It's a longer drop than I realised," I said, trying not to picture Marina's fall.

"Yes," he said simply.

We stood still for a moment before I spoke again.

"I guess when fitted with sails it would have been almost as good a landmark for sailors as a lighthouse, during the daytime, at least. I wonder how far away you can see it?"

I tried to pull my hand free from his as I turned to look out to sea, but he didn't let go. There were still no pleasure boats plying the waters.

I'd had enough.

"I bet Katerina's group is back from the windmill by now. Let's go back and compare notes."

He looked at me for a moment, and I had no idea what he was thinking. Then he nodded.

"OK, Sophie, let's go."

As we left the water, he dropped my hand and continued as if nothing had happened between us. We returned to the hotel with me feeling increasingly uncomfortable in his presence.

24 In the Picture

The weather had warmed up sufficiently for us to welcome *café frappés* when we gathered by the pool to compare notes on our findings.

"On the hill we saw nothing but goats," reported Katerina, whose party had, unsurprisingly, been first to complete its mission.

Cecilia and Stacey had taken rather longer. They'd headed first to the shop to call for Ariadne. She'd guided them into the ruined houses along the shoreline, giving a running commentary on who had lived in each, their character foibles and their ancestors, and where they had fled after the earthquake. Only her family had stayed on, her grandmother too frail to withstand the journey to the mainland, maintaining the shop they'd run for generations. Slowly it morphed from a grocery store to a souvenir shop as the nature of the local traffic changed from fishing boats to tourist pleasure craft, including hobbyists in small yachts, like Dominic's father, and shallow draught day trippers' boats from Lefkas. The waters were too shallow to permit larger vessels – a mixed blessing, as although their trade would have boosted

Ariadne's takings, and Katerina's too, it might have spoiled much of what was special about Floros.

Returning to the shop, gratified by her appreciative audience, Ariadne had shared a big bottle of iced tea with Cecilia and Stacey. Then while Stacey, feeling a bit sunburnt, had applied some suncream, Ariadne had given Cecilia a tour of her little house and its ramshackle array of outhouses that served as stockroom, distillery and tiny island museum, a jackdaw-like collection of items left behind by earthquake emigrants. Of Marina there was no sign.

Ben reported on our search.

"It was refreshing to see a coast free of litter and plastic." He had written newspaper features about marine pollution. "Although I guess soon there'll be a solitary blue flip-flop floating on the waves, when it gets blown down from the ledge beneath the cliff."

I'd rather have found a flip-flop than Marina's dead body, but I kept that to myself.

I was not surprised to hear the party searching Windmill Hill had found nothing new, but had higher hopes of the others, covering fresh ground across the top of the island.

Vasili, Dominic and Lydia had been the last back to the hotel, their route the longest and steepest. Lydia had slowed their pace as they approached to collect a bunch of wild flowers along the way.

"Back home, that would be against the law," I said, coveting her fragrant posy. "The countryside code says we should leave everywhere as we find it."

Lydia shrugged. "If I left all these where I found them, they'd only get eaten by goats."

Vasili grinned. "This is Greece."

"This is Floros," echoed Katerina.

Ben turned his notebook to a fresh page.

"So what did you guys find, Vasili?"

While Vasili filed his report, Katerina went to make another round of *frappés* for us all. We'd certainly have no problem staying alert for our postponed afternoon class.

"We found nothing helpful, only a reminder to myself of how steep the path is to the monastery, which might be a clue in itself. If by some chance, she didn't fall off the cliff, but just dropped her phone by accident and went elsewhere, I don't think Marina would have gone that way. Too hard for her, even in thongs."

"In *what*?" asked Dominic.

"We call flip-flops thongs in Australia," said Vasili, gathering up the empty coffee glasses from the first round.

Dominic shuddered. "Don't make me picture Marina in a thong."

"I guess there's nothing more we can do until the police arrive," said Ben, closing his notebook and setting it down on the table. "Anyone mind if I take a few photos of the group in the meantime? Lydia, you first, with those wild flowers."

I hoped he wasn't planning a caption suggesting a memorial bouquet for Marina. I thought it best to drop the others a hint about Ben's ulterior motive.

"Don't forget to sign release forms, folks, if you're happy for Ben to use any of your pictures in his paper."

Cecilia, Kimberley and Dawn shrank back, making excuses not to pose. The men, however, seemed entirely game. Tristram coughed, self-importantly.

"Make sure you describe me as Tristram DeVere, entrepreneur, capital D, capital V, no space between."

Dominic leaned forward to write his own name in block capitals on Ben's pad.

"And spell my surname right, please," he added. "Don't forget the hyphen between the Blackwood and the Smythe with a y and an e. You can't imagine how often I get called Blacksmith by mistake."

Cecilia grinned. "Or on purpose by socialists."

"As soon as you're done, let's get down to work," said Stacey. "Katerina, please could we have our lunch out here on the terrace and work through to make up for losing time this morning? Sandwiches will do."

Katerina acquiesced. "Of course, Stacey."

Both must have been conscious of the need for business as usual, for the sake of the hotel and the seven remaining retreats.

As we went to fetch our notebooks from our rooms, I tried to frame an appropriate comment for the course feedback form that Stacey had already distributed. She might have to provide continuation sheets.

***

"Now, today we're going to talk about writing productivity," began Stacey.

The sun was really bright now, what little remained of the storm winds sending any clouds scudding westwards towards Italy.

"First, I want to debunk the myth of writer's block, which is a much-cited hurdle, especially for beginners."

"That's no myth, I get it all the time," said Tristram. "Why do you think my memoir's got stuck at my childhood?"

Stacey levelled her gaze at him. "In my view, writer's block simply means you are trying to write the wrong thing."

"Well, who else's memoirs am I meant to write? Richard Branson's?"

He almost spat the name out. Stacey, seated next to him, laid a hand on his forearm.

"But what's holding you back, Tristram? I haven't noticed any lack of facility with words in conversation. You're very articulate."

"I should say so. My secretary told me I'm quite unusual, because when I dictate letters or reports, they come out in coherent, grammatical sentences, without hesitation."

"There, you see?" Stacey clapped her hands together in triumph. "That's your comfort zone: writing not about yourself, but about your business. Don't answer me now – I don't want to put you on the spot – but please consider whether there's a different book you'd rather be writing, in which you disregard your personal life, or at least cite only the occasional personal anecdote, but expound on your business theories. A how-to book, not a memoir."

Tristram opened his mouth to speak, but then closed it again, deep in thought.

"I could write about myself till kingdom come," said Lydia brightly. "Look, I've even started writing a character sketch of myself to put in my play."

Stacey looked wary. "Is the play going to be autobiographical?"

Lydia wrinkled her nose.

"Not really. I just think I'd be the right sort of personality for the protagonist. Then if it ever gets produced, I'll be the obvious person to cast in the lead. I won't even have to audition. Or act!"

When she laughed at her own joke, Dominic smiled indulgently. With her good looks and flirtatious manner,

I bet she never had any trouble getting parts. She'd certainly liven up the Wendlebury Players back in my home village.

Cecilia sat forward in her chair, her face full of mischief.

"I'd love to read that character sketch of yours. May I?"

Lydia welcomed her interest.

"Sure. It's on the first page."

She handed Cecilia her black spiral-bound pad, and Cecilia sat back to enjoy it. But when she opened the book, her eyes widened in surprise.

"I didn't think you meant that sort of sketch."

She held it up for us to see. Filling the page was a large pencil sketch of Lydia, undressed and lying on a bed among rumpled sheets. She must have copied it from a photograph. Dominic grinned proudly.

"I don't know, I think it sums her up pretty well."

Lydia was unabashed.

"Sorry, wrong notebook. Let me pop up to my room to fetch the other one. They've both got the same binding, only that one's got art paper, the other's ruled. It's a wonder I haven't muddled them up before."

With a parting giggle at her own daffiness, she trotted back inside. Cecilia couldn't resist flicking through the rest of the sketchpad.

"Oh, look at this!"

She held up a watercolour for us all to see, a view from Lydia's balcony across to Windmill Hill. As the room on the end of the building, Lydia's was the only one from which you could see the plateau, if you leaned over the railing and looked round the corner. As far as I knew, none of us besides Dominic had been on her balcony, so

154

we were all interested in seeing the now familiar setting of Marina's disappearance from a new angle.

"Look, that must be Marina." Kimberley pointed at the figure on the track in a blue sarong. "But who's that on top of the plateau with her?"

Between Marina and the windmill was a man's figure in a blue short-sleeved shirt and beige shorts. His hair was a blur of brown, but more detail was impossible to make out as Lydia's painting style was impressionistic, and the people in the painting far away.

"Which of you guys has a blue shirt and beige shorts?" Cecilia looked from Ben to Dominic to Tristram. Each raised a hand.

A clink of glasses behind us heralded Vasili's appearance. He was bearing a tray of sandwiches – and wearing a blue shirt and beige shorts, the kind that zip off at the knee from long trousers. He must have wondered why we were staring at him.

Tristram folded his arms across his chest.

"Well, what self-respecting man in the Med in summer doesn't have a pair of beige chinos and a light-blue short-sleeved shirt?"

"Ionian," said Dominic automatically.

"I blame Attenborough," said Dawn. "He always wears that colour combination when filming."

Dominic huffed. "Much as I love Sir David, I wouldn't defer to him as a fashion icon."

A patter of bare feet heralded Lydia's return, bearing her other notebook. She pouted when she saw her sketchbook open on Cecilia's lap at the landscape. I was glad she hadn't meant to share her self-portrait. She did have some degree of modesty.

Cecilia quickly placated her.

"They're very good pictures, Lydia. You're a talented artist. Have you done all these since we got here?"

"Yes. It would have been weird if I'd done them beforehand. I mean, I'm not psychic or anything."

She giggled.

I pointed to one of the figures in the painting.

"That looks like Marina, so you must have done it before she disappeared. The other one looks like a man. Who could that be? And why didn't you tell us about this picture before, when Marina went missing?"

Suddenly I remembered the pale man I'd seen by Ariadne's shop. But I wasn't going to mention him until the men in our party had been accounted for. A mysterious stranger might provide a convenient scapegoat for the genuinely guilty person. I didn't want to falsely incriminate a monk on his day off.

Lydia scrutinised the sketch for a moment.

"How should I know? Does it matter? It's only a sketch, not a portrait."

Ben came to her defence.

"Yes, it's hardly evidence, Sophie. It's not like a photograph or a police identikit picture. She could just have painted him in from her imagination, for balance in the composition. Like poetic licence, only in watercolour."

Lydia tapped her forehead with her pencil.

"Yes, that's exactly what I do. Thanks, Ben."

I moved Cecilia's hand aside to reveal the date of Lydia's signature.

"What time of day did you paint this exactly?"

Lydia thought for a moment. "After lunch, when everyone else was having a siesta."

"Marina wasn't," I said. "Nor was I. Do you remember whether it was a real man, Lydia? And if so, any idea which of our party it was?"

She shrugged. "No idea. I'm an artist, not a private detective."

The men exchanged glances, each waiting for one of the others to be first to speak.

"I don't recall leaving the hotel grounds that afternoon," said Ben. "I had a siesta and a swim, and then I spent a few hours writing on my balcony, and then it was suppertime."

Dominic nodded. "Same here. No witness to my siesta, though. Unlike Sunday's." He smiled awkwardly.

Tristram frowned. "I went to my room but didn't sleep. I reread what I've written so far of my memoir, and that took all afternoon."

Stacey's mouth fell open. "Really, the whole afternoon? Just how much have you written?"

"About a hundred pages of A4."

"And so far you're six years old?"

"I have a very good memory."

Vasili, concentrating on collecting our empty coffee glasses, said nothing, so I prompted him.

"Vasili? Did you go up on Windmill Hill at all on Monday afternoon?"

Vasili set down his tray to count his tasks off on his fingers.

"I cleaned my boat after lunch, then I helped my grandmother in her shop for a while. She needed some heavy boxes brought in from her storeroom and I unpacked them for her, so she could price-mark and shelve them. Then I chopped some firewood for her oven and milked her goat."

This was the boy his mother called lazy.

157

"But the hill? Did you go up Windmill Hill?"

"No."

"Then who was it?"

The men all looked at each other again as if expecting someone to confess. I was about to put them out of their misery by mentioning the stranger, when Lydia decided to get stroppy.

"Does it really matter so much? I mean, it's not as if I'm going to sell or publish the picture. I'm not like Ben. I don't need release forms to put someone in a picture, do I?"

When nobody stepped in to defend her, Lydia lost patience.

"Oh, for goodness' sake, why don't any of you want it to be you in my picture? You ought to be pleased to be painted. I know I would be."

Dominic put a hand on her knee to show moral support, but she pushed it away crossly.

"You're all pathetic," she snapped. "I'm going up the hill to text my husband."

She threw her notebook on to the coffee table with such force that the crockery juddered, as if shaken by an earth tremor. I wondered, not for the first time since our arrival, what the chances were of another earthquake on the island.

Stacey put her head in her hands.

"I hope to goodness she's not going to get him to complain about the course."

Ben closed his reporters' notebook, then froze.

"You don't suppose she'll tell him about Marina's disappearance, do you?"

Stacey raised her face. "God, I hope not. Didn't we all agree not to let this get out until we've informed Marina's next of kin? You are all OK about that, aren't you?"

She looked at each of us in turn, her eyes pleading. Ben, bent on his scoop, nodded vigorously. Cecilia laid a comforting hand on Stacey's arm.

"I don't envy you that task."

Stacey grimaced. "Actually, I thought we should get the police to do it, once they get here. It's their job really, not mine. I hope they speak good English. It would be ghastly if the message got lost in translation."

"I'm sure Vasili can help if need be," I said, wondering why Cecilia didn't volunteer. A middle-aged woman's voice would be more comforting and appropriate than a young man with an Aussie accent. "Any news on their ETA, Vasili?"

"My father will be here tomorrow for sure." Vasili raised his face to the sun. "See, the weather is gorgeous now. All is calm. I'll fetch him from the mainland in my boat at first light."

I shouldered my handbag and stood up. "I think I'd better follow Lydia and make sure she doesn't go blurting the news about Marina out to her husband."

I'd have found it hard not to tell Hector, so I was glad I had decided not to phone him since Marina's disappearance.

Stacey had given up on an afternoon session by this stage. "So much for productivity," she murmured as I made my way towards the gate.

***

On reaching the plateau, I discovered Lydia lying on her back, arms and legs stretched out to sunbathe, a blade of grass in her mouth. She'd lowered her sun hat over her eyes, but either she was peeking through the gaps in the straw or she recognised my footfall.

159

"What do you want, Sophie?"

I knelt down on the warm ground beside her, releasing the astringent fragrance of tight little tufts of thyme growing among the grass. I planned to plant more thyme in my garden when I got home.

"Have you just been texting your husband?"

She didn't move.

"What's it to you?"

I took a deep breath to stop myself snapping back at her in the same tone.

"I just wanted to ask you, on behalf of Stacey and Katerina, not to tell him yet about Marina's disappearance. Not till the police have been, anyway."

"Why shouldn't I?"

"Her next of kin don't know yet. Can you imagine how awful it would be if they heard it first from the papers? You wouldn't like to be responsible for upsetting her bereaved family, would you?"

She pulled her hat off her face to look me in the eye.

"Don't patronise me, Sophie, I'm not stupid. For goodness' sake, I'm old enough to be your sister."

I couldn't argue with that.

"Besides, you've no need to worry about me telling Bob. I haven't spoken to him since Sunday anyway."

"Really? I thought you were meant to phone him every day?"

She slid her hat back over her face.

"Well, he can't make me. Not while I'm here. I'm having too much fun, making the most of my freedom while I'm shot of him. I'll have to go back all too soon as it is. I'm amazed he's not kicking up a rumpus already about me not phoning, but I'll just tell him it's the signal and beyond my control. I'll have to face the music when

I get home. It's a pain, but I know how to make him forgive me. Goodness knows, I've had enough practice."

She raised her hands and stretched out her fingers.

"I didn't even bring my phone up here with me. I just wanted some space away from the rest of you. And now you've spoiled it."

She rolled over on to her stomach, knelt up, then rose to her feet.

"I'm out of here. If you want to hang around for fun, you're welcome to it."

She strolled off down the track, leaving me wondering what to do next.

Hector. I really did need to phone Hector. I pulled my phone from my handbag and this time was able to make a quick connection. The clearer weather might have improved the signal.

"Hector. It's me. Have you got a minute? There's something I need to ask you, in strictest confidence."

***

Twenty minutes later, I was strolling back down the track to the hotel when Vasili turned out of the gate and started towards me. He was carrying on his arm a basket of bread, cakes, fruit, and a couple of bottles of water. At the sight of me, he made as if to retrace his steps, but realising I'd seen him too, he thought better of it.

"You off for a picnic, Vasili?" I asked. It seemed unlikely when we'd already had an excursion today, followed by a lunch of deep-filled sandwiches, fruit and cake.

"Oh. Yes, yes, that's it."

He could tell I wasn't convinced, so he tried again.

161

"Actually, I'm taking some provisions to my grandmother."

I grinned. "Quite the Little Red Riding Hood. Look out for the Big Bad Wolf."

He bared his teeth and raised his free hand, curling his fingers to imitate wolf-like claws.

I couldn't understand why he'd be taking the bottles of water to his grandmother when she stocked them in her shop. I was therefore not surprised, but I was puzzled, when I turned round on reaching the hotel gate to see Vasili was now walking up the track to Windmill Hill.

25 Productive Thinking

Supper was a desultory affair, despite Katerina's generous servings of a herby lamb casserole, redolent of garlic. Stacey gamely tried to launch a conversation about productivity to follow on from our curtailed afternoon session, but only Kimberley bothered to answer any of her questions, and it soon petered out into a monologue. I tried to show willing by taking notes – she'd asked us all to bring our notebooks to the table to catch up – but my mind drifted, and between mouthfuls of the delicious meal, I found myself reliving my earlier telephone conversation with Hector.

"'Once you eliminate the impossible, whatever remains, no matter how improbable, must be the truth'," he'd advised.

"That's all very well for you to say," I objected.

"It wasn't me. I was quoting Sherlock Holmes."

"I expect Sherlock Holmes would deduce it was a mad monk. Doesn't he dress up as a Greek orthodox monk in one of his stories?"

"You're thinking of the Italian clergyman in *The Final Problem*. But I bet he'd relish dressing up as a monk to infiltrate a monastery. Now there's an idea for fan fiction.

Anyway, what makes you assume it was a man? Apart from the monks, there are more women than men on the island, aren't there?"

"Yes, but there is one that you don't know about. I didn't tell you about the strange man lurking by the shop the other day. He looked a bit pale to be a local, but then I guess the monks spend too much time indoors to work up a tan – I assumed he might be a monk on his day off. No-one else has mentioned him, and I'm beginning to think I dreamt him. The only other place he's pitched up is in one of Lydia's pictures. Possibly. She painted a man in shorts, though only as a speck in the distance, and of course all the men wear shorts in this heat, even during the storm."

"Women can wear shorts as well as men. I can't believe your feminist friend Cecilia didn't point that out."

"Maybe Cecilia killed Marina."

"Or Lydia. It sounds to me as if she's not as daft as she makes out. Is she clever enough to have painted in a man as a red herring? Besides, you only have her word for it that she painted the picture in real time, as Marina was about to fall to her death. She could have painted it at any time since. Watercolours must dry fast out there."

Was Lydia that cunning? I looked across the table to see her picking her paper napkin apart then trickling the resulting confetti into Dominic's hair. Cunning or not, she didn't seem troubled by her conscience.

Stacey was still holding forth about writing habits.

"It's not the number of words you write per day that matters, but the regularity. Graham Greene aimed for just five hundred. You don't even need to write every day. Sometimes you'll need days to concentrate on editing, or planning your next book, or to take time out to replenish the creative well. They all use different parts of your brain."

Dominic brushed the latest delivery of confetti from his hair on to his empty plate.

"I'm not sure I've got enough parts of my brain to go round for this writing lark."

As Vasili whisked away our plates, Katerina arrived with a tray of tiny Greek pastries, oozing honey and cinnamon, and a stone pot of thick, glossy yoghurt with a pottery ladle. She looked surprisingly cheerful, then she explained why.

"My husband, he comes tomorrow. He is not often on Floros in tourist time."

Katerina's life couldn't have been as idyllic as its setting suggested. She had sacrificed a great deal to remain here. I wondered whether she'd ever spent time away from Floros herself – not much, for sure. It was a miracle she was as sane and sensible as she appeared.

***

As I lay in bed that night, unable to sleep, I looked forward to the arrival of Katerina's husband and the imposition of formal law and order. In darker moments, our situation reminded me of my GCSE English set book: William Golding's *Lord of the Flies*. Memories of the story chilled me still. It would have been quite a different book if there'd been girls on that plane.

As I turned over, I caught sight of my travel journal open on my desk. I'd forgotten to write that day's entry. I threw back the sheet, fetched a glass of water from the bathroom, and made myself comfortable at the desk. I had an awful lot to catch up on.

I wrote until gone 2am, enjoying the refreshing night air drifting in through the mosquito screen over the balcony doors. Consequently, I didn't wake up till half past breakfast time. After throwing on a sundress and brushing my teeth with one hand and my hair with the other (not easy), I ran down the corridor and the stairs to arrive breathless at the dining room.

Everyone stared at me as I sat down and grabbed a croissant. I was famished. All these generous Greek meals were stretching my stomach.

"Oh good, I'm glad you're alright," said Cecilia, pouring me a coffee. "I don't suppose you saw Lydia on your way down, did you? Her room's next to yours, isn't it?"

A glance around the table told me Lydia was absent.

"No, sorry. I didn't hear any signs of life."

A stupid phrase to use in the circumstances. I was sorry as soon as I'd said it. Feeling Dominic's eyes upon me, I blushed, wondering whether he thought I'd been listening in to their antics. I countered with a quizzical look.

"No, Sophie, I haven't seen her either, not since supper."

The lead in Ben's pencil snapped as he pressed a little too hard on his shorthand pad. He looked up.

"Has anyone?"

Silence.

I lay down the rest of my croissant, no longer hungry.

"Maybe she's painting on her balcony and lost track of time – or working on her play."

I convinced no-one, least of all myself.

"I'll go back upstairs and give her a knock. She's probably just overslept, like I did."

I scraped back my chair and fled, heart pounding. No wonder the silence in the night had kept me awake. Perhaps I'd known deep down something was wrong.

***

"Let me go and break the door down."

Dominic, pale and clammy, lowered his coffee cup, spilling brown drops on to his saucer.

"Don't be too hasty, Dominic," I said. "She may just be too deeply asleep to have heard my knock."

Dominic acted as if I hadn't spoken.

"Call the police," he said automatically.

"But we don't have to," said Stacey. "Katerina's husband has just arrived."

"Then where the hell is he?" Dominic threw down his napkin and strode out into the lobby, where he pressed the bell on the desk seven times. Ben and I followed him.

"She's probably fine," I assured him. "But let's go and ask Katerina for Lydia's room key and we'll check."

Ben started to sharpen his pencil into an ashtray on the counter with a small Swiss army knife. He could have done with a propelling pencil.

Katerina emerged from the kitchen, smiling and placid. Through the swing door I could hear lively conversation in Greek between Vasili and another man of deeper, gruffer voice, presumably his father. Their combative tone reminded me of Kostas, our taxi driver.

Katerina straightened the bell that Dominic had disturbed.

"Hello, Dominic. How can I help?"

"Find Lydia."

"Why, is she lost?"

"She's not come down to breakfast."

167

"Maybe she's not hungry."

I leaned forward.

"Katerina, please may I borrow your spare key to Lydia's room? She's probably just sound asleep after all the excitement yesterday, but I would like to check on her to put our minds at rest."

In silence, Katerina passed me the key from the numbered pigeonhole behind the desk – not the most secure system in the world – and I headed for the stairs.

Cecilia followed in my wake.

"I thought you might be glad of reinforcements if you find anything untoward," she said as we entered the corridor leading to the bedrooms.

"Thanks, Cecilia. Let's hope that won't be necessary."

We reached Lydia's room. As I turned the key in the lock, I called out from the threshold: "Lydia! It's only me and Cecilia! Wake up! Are you OK? It's getting late. We're worried about you."

Receiving no response, we ventured inside, fearing the worst, but finding only a neatly made bed bearing the hallmarks of Katerina's daily service, with Lydia's towel folded into the shape of a swan. Last night's wrapped chocolate still lay untouched on the pillow.

On the desk lay Lydia's open sketchbook, as if she'd downed tools halfway through a drawing. This time she was painting not the view from her balcony, but a photograph propped up by the desk lamp. The photo showed a pale-skinned man of about forty, with short greying hair and round silver-rimmed glasses, wearing a blue shirt and buff shorts. I didn't dare touch it, for fear of leaving fingerprints, though I longed to check the back for an inscription. I was willing to bet that this was a photo of her husband.

I looked around for her handbag. It was gone.

I turned to Cecilia.

"Katerina's husband has arrived not a moment too soon. We have a second disappearance for him to investigate. Let's get back downstairs and fill him in."

26 Enter Vasilios

Katerina was waiting at the reception desk for our return, emptying Ben's pencil sharpenings into her bin.

"Well?"

I leaned on the desk and tried to keep my voice calm and even for the sake of her nerves.

"Lydia's bed hasn't been slept in and her handbag's gone. It looks to me as if she went out late last night and hasn't returned."

"Oh no, that cannot be!"

"I don't know what else to think, Katerina. None of us has seen her."

"Not even Dominic," added Cecilia.

"It is a good thing my husband is here at last. He will take care of it for you. I am sure he will know what to do." Being married to a policeman would have its advantages. "Would you like to come and meet him?"

When Katerina beckoned to us, we followed her into the kitchen, where a stocky middle-aged man in Greek police uniform stood up respectfully and flashed a charming smile. With his dark eyes, thick salt-and-pepper curls and five o'clock shadow even at this early hour, he was clearly Vasili's father, despite being significantly shorter. Katerina was smaller still, though at least six inches taller than Ariadne.

"Ladies, this is my husband, Vasilios."

Katerina gazed at him fondly. For a girl living on a nearly deserted island, he must have been quite a catch. Her mother must have been very pleased for her to marry so well without her new husband whisking her away to the mainland.

I stepped forward to shake his hand.

"Vasilios, I am so glad you are here," I said. "And not a moment too soon."

Vasilios's big brown eyes widened a little, his smile unfaltering as he glanced sideways to Katerina in a silent appeal for help.

"Oh, I'm sorry." I put my hand to my mouth. "*Sighnomi*. I don't speak Greek. But Cecilia does, don't you, Cecilia? She will translate."

Before I'd finished the sentence, at my back came the dull thud of the swing door, and when I looked round, Cecilia was nowhere to be seen.

"Vasili!" roared Vasilios, still beaming.

Vasili strolled in through the swing door with a tray of dirty breakfast dishes balanced elegantly on one hand. Perhaps he was trying to hone his skills to escape to a more glamorous waiting job on the mainland.

"*Ne, Baba?*"

There followed a flurry of Greek words filled with passion. By the end of his tirade, Vasilios was red in the face.

Vasili turned to me calmly.

"My *baba* – I mean, my dad – has asked me to translate for you guys. No worries, hey, Mama?"

Katerina shook her head.

"But first, Vasili, did you see where Cecilia went just now?" I asked. "She ran off for no apparent reason."

Vasili handed the tray to Katerina.

"She went outside. I thought someone had upset her. But I don't know who. The rest of the gang, bar Marina and Lydia, are still in the dining room."

Katerina paled and set down the tray by the dishwasher, rattling the crockery.

"She ran away as soon as she saw my husband, Sophie. Do you think she is guilty one?"

I didn't dare answer for fear of incriminating Cecilia, but nor did I want to pervert the course of justice. I went to put my arm around Katerina.

"I think it's time for us to let the authorities take charge."

I turned to her son.

"Vasili, please bring your father through to the dining room and help us tell him what we know."

***

Having to go through a translator slowed down the process, but on the plus side it gave us more time to gather our thoughts between exchanges. The delay encouraged us to speak rationally rather than emotionally.

Vasilios seemed excited to have a possible murder case to investigate, plus the bonus of a disappearance. There can't have been many cases of serious crime on Floros, or even on Ithaca as a whole. Ithaca, with its small population (just 3,000, according to a leaflet I'd picked up in the lobby), had a village atmosphere. Just as in Wendlebury Barrow, fewer crimes would be committed than in a more anonymous urban community because everyone would know everyone else.

Poor Vasilios probably spent most of his life dealing with traffic accidents and drunken tourists. Now here he was handling a crime involving a world-famous author. His name might even end up in newspapers around the world, whether or not he solved the case. Certainly Ben lost no time in photographing Vasilios for his precious scoop, and Vasilios was happy to sign Ben's photographic release form. He drew in an extra box on which to write his rank.

As Vasilios continued his questioning, Katerina, bringing in a fresh tray of coffees, looked proud of her husband. It may have been the first time she'd seen him in action on a serious case. After a while, she sat down beside him to admire the spectacle.

Vasilios tapped all of our observations into his tablet, nodding approval. Then he sat back and folded his hands in his lap, as if the case was already done and dusted. Next he fired off a few rapid sentences to Vasili, who delivered the translation.

"My father says we have done well to search the island, but he thinks he knows one place we haven't looked."

Dominic thumped his fist on the table, rattling the cups.

"We haven't looked anywhere for Lydia yet. When are we going to start looking for her?"

Vasili translated again for his father before giving his reply.

"My father says Lydia has not been missing long enough to be an official missing person. You will probably find her sunbathing by the pool. Maybe she just went for a walk. He says young girls skip breakfast every day to keep slim for their sweethearts."

I was glad Cecilia wasn't there to hear that piece of chauvinism.

Dominic leapt to his feet and stormed out of the door to the terrace. We could hear him crashing about between chairs and sunbeds and umbrellas and heaving open the door of the maintenance shed that was usually the preserve of Vasili.

"No screams yet, so I guess she's not lying drowned in the pool," said Ben calmly, scribbling on his pad.

Dawn upset her coffee cup in anguish.

"For goodness' sake, Ben, how can you be so callous? I suppose you'd like a grisly story of a pretty English holidaymaker's death by misadventure? That'd score you a few points with your editor."

"Well, she was pretty drunk last night."

As if that was a defence! It was my turn to admonish Ben.

"If you honestly expected that to be the outcome, why weren't you checking up on Lydia last night?"

I wrapped my arms across my chest for comfort. Were all newspaper reporters this cold-blooded in the face of tragedy?

"I'd have thought that was down to Dominic," retorted Ben. But he had the decency to look abashed as Dominic slouched back into the room and slumped into a chair.

"OK, let's go look further afield," he said. "With any luck, the policeman's right, and she's just gone to the windmill with her phone."

"But her bed wasn't slept in," I pointed out. "The swan and the chocolate were still on her pillow from last night."

Ben shrugged.

"Surely it's not beyond her abilities to make her own bed and fold her towel to save Katerina the trouble."

Stacey shook her head. "Making the bed, maybe, but folding her towel back into a swan? And not eating the chocolate?"

"Wait a minute!" I raised my hand. "In Lydia's bedroom just now I found a portrait of a man." I looked around for Cecilia's concurrence, but of course she wasn't there.

"Not that tiresome portrait of the mysterious man in shorts again?" Ben laid down his pencil. "You can show that to Vasilios but he'll probably think it's a picture of himself. His uniform shirt is pale blue."

I frowned at his impatience. "No, this was a new picture, a portrait she was copying from a photograph. A pale grey-haired man. I'm pretty sure it was her husband."

Vasilios coughed, and we had to wait while Vasili caught his father up with our conversation. Once Vasilios had stopped tapping all of this into his tablet, he looked up hopefully, and Ben continued.

"So what's Lydia's husband got to do with it?"

Dominic turned away from us in his seat, suddenly fascinated by his fingernails.

Ben pointed his pencil at me. "Her husband's back in England, in receipt of a barrage of affectionate texts. How is he relevant?"

I wondered how Dominic would take my announcement.

"Actually, I think he's here on the island."

Dominic's mouth fell open.

"How can that be? There's nowhere for him to stay except here, and we're Katerina's only guests. Aren't we, Katerina?"

Katerina fidgeted in her seat.

"Of course."

I raised my hand.

"No. There is another place. Ariadne's house. She has a guest room and outhouses. Cecilia told me she'd checked them when we were searching the seashore for Marina."

Kimberley came to Ariadne's defence.

"But Cecilia said Ariadne's guest room's full of boxes of souvenir tea towels and such, and her outhouses are used as stores of wine and olive oil. There's no-one living in there."

I was reluctant to say it, but I had to.

"We only have Cecilia's word for that, and she's not here to ask. In the absence of any proof to the contrary, we have to assume it could be a possibility. You see, I'm sure I saw a strange man at the side of her house on Monday, and he looked just like the man in Lydia's painting."

Dominic drained his coffee cup.

"That's ridiculous, Sophie. If he was her husband, don't you think he'd have come up to see her rather than skulking down by the harbour?"

Vasili refilled Dominic's cup. If he'd offered something stronger, I think Dominic would have accepted it.

Then Vasili winked. "All you Englishmen look the same. It was probably just some guy left behind by the day trippers' boat on Sunday. That was the last time it landed here. Poor guy would have been really stuck, as the storm would have prevented them rescuing him. The crew on that boat are rogues. They're meant to count passengers off and on again at every stop. But you'd think they'd never learned to count, the number of people they leave behind. I wouldn't mind so much if they asked me to taxi their castaways home, but no, it is always their cousin or their brother or their uncle who they send to fetch them."

Katerina tutted. "Swordfish, nothing but swordfish."

"Swordfish?"

"Those boatmen are only interested in the girl tourists, just like the worst of the waiters on the mainland. They not care about the men. Not like my Vasili. He's a good boy." Vasili glowed beneath her rare praise. "The tourist police should be checking up on them, not on hotel owners like us."

I turned to Vasilios. "Are you a tourist policeman?"

Vasili replied on his behalf without translating.

"Don't worry, my dad's the real thing. The tourist police are what you might call a tourist authority in England. They're not exactly armed guards; they just try to enforce standards in tourism."

So Cecilia, in league with Ariadne, might be hiding Lydia's husband in the shop. And perhaps now Lydia too. But why?

27 To the Windmill

"If you insist, Sophie, my father can search my grandmother's house again," said Vasili. "But she won't be pleased."

It was natural that Vasili should be defensive of his grandmother, and I was loath to offend any of his family. I tried to look on the bright side.

"At least if Lydia is there, she'll be safe."

Ben grinned at Dominic.

"Although if her husband's there, I don't rate your chances much, mate."

"Actually, my father is in charge, and he still says Lydia is not the missing person. Marina is. You may be a bunch of authors, but he is the authority on the island now. Geddit?" Vasili was enjoying this far too much for my liking.

"So, what are we meant to do?" asked Stacey, looking at her watch. "Just leave him to it and get on with our course – which I admit would be my preference – or does he want us to help?"

Vasili and his father conversed at length in Greek. Then Vasili turned back to us.

"He said there is one place we haven't looked for Marina, and until that place has been checked, that is his priority."

"But we looked in every building on the island apart from the monastery," said Kimberley. "Surely he's not going to raid the monastery?"

Katerina and Vasili crossed themselves, and so did Vasilios after a nudge and a whisper from his wife.

"No, we didn't," I suddenly realised. "There's another place too. We didn't go inside the windmill."

"But we've already talked about this – the door's boarded up," said Stacey. "How could Marina get in there to hide, and then board up the door from the outside?"

I remembered running my fingers over the dry old driftwood boards, nails rusted into them, eroded by the salty winds off the sea. Perhaps they'd been there since the earthquake.

"But who said there's only one door? Mightn't a windmill have a back and a front door like a house? There could be a back door out of sight from where we've been standing, facing the cliff edge, which still opens."

They all looked at me while this sank in. Katerina paled, reeled slightly in her seat. Vasili reached out to squeeze his mother's hand as he gabbled a quick summary to his father. Vasilios looked to his wife for approval and she gave a scarcely perceptible nod.

"OK, we go up there now to see," said Katerina slowly. "You go, I stay. Just in case Lydia comes back from her walk and needs anything."

"Or Cecilia," added Stacey.

"Cecilia?" asked Vasilios, and for a moment I wondered whether he could understand English after all.

Vasili reached out a hand to me. "Sophie, my father says you must come, and you, Ben, because you were the ones who discovered Marina's apparent fall. Then you can show him the evidence and tell him everything in your own words."

Or in *your* own words, I thought, hoping Vasili's translation was accurate. His English was faultless, but how blameless were his motives?

28 Grist to the Mill

Vasili trudged ahead of Ben and me to keep pace with his father, chatting in Greek all the way. I was feeling increasingly isolated, as if it was us versus them, tourists versus Greeks – but I didn't know whether to trust Ben either.

As we neared the windmill in glorious sunshine, the storm long gone, we slowed our pace, perhaps subconsciously reluctant to encounter any painful revelations before we had to. I pointed to the rusty nails in the boards across the door.

"You see? This has been nailed up for ages. But what lies hidden round the back?"

Vasilios strode past me towards the cliff, rounding the base of the windmill with the enigmatic smile of a detective about to call everyone into the library to unmask the murderer.

"Be careful!" I called as he disappeared around the base of the building, treading perilously close to the cliff edge.

Vasili followed, calling over his shoulder: "Don't worry, we're safe as –"

The end of his sentence was muffled by the windmill's bulk between us. I hoped it wouldn't be a case of famous last words.

Then one hand reappeared – Vasili's – holding out an empty basket, tantalisingly, like a burlesque dancer offering an undergarment, before he brought it out to place on the ground in front of us. Forgetting about my safety, I stepped forward to take it from him.

"I've seen that basket before," I cried. "I saw you carrying it up here yesterday full of food – including things Ariadne would have in her shop. So, it wasn't for Ariadne, but for someone else holed up in the windmill?"

Without answering, Vasili disappeared around the back of the building again. A brief conversation between father and son, then Vasili called out in English, "Marina, it's me. It's all up now. Please open the door and we'll take you back to the hotel. It's Day 5, like we agreed. You have two days left to make up for lost time to the delegates."

He came back round to the front of the windmill.

My mouth dropped open. "Like you agreed? Vasili, don't tell me you knew about this all along? You mean Marina didn't fall off the cliff at all? Didn't fall and wasn't pushed, but was enjoying a secret retreat alone in a windmill?"

Ben flashed a conspiratorial look at Vasili before addressing me: "Well done, Sherlock."

"Well, Marina did come for a writer's retreat, didn't she?" said Vasili, grinning. "Before she arrived, her agent wrote to ask my mother – who, as you know, is her greatest fan – for a private place to stay where she wouldn't be bothered by any of you."

I folded my arms across my chest. "Well, there's a nerve! We've all paid hundreds of pounds to spend a week being inspired by a famous novelist, and she does a runner? How selfish is that?"

Ben coughed. "Well, you didn't pay, did you?"

I frowned. "No, but everyone else did. Having someone famous here was part of the attraction for paying participants. Stacey will be incensed. Your thoughtless, selfish plan has ruined her retreat, and possibly her business, her reputation and her career."

I shook my fist at Vasili.

"I knew there was something odd about that basket of food you claimed you were taking to Ariadne. All along it was room service for Marina. And as for involving the police – well, this is all just a game to your father, isn't it? An excuse to take a midweek trip home?"

From behind the windmill came a more frantic knocking. Then Vasilios emerged, deathly pale, and said something unusually succinct to his son. Vasili turned to us, wide-eyed.

"My father says Marina did not reply. But he can hear a man and a woman arguing inside."

I stepped up to the windmill and pressed my ear against the boarded-up door. I couldn't hear a thing.

"My father says you need to go further round the back, where there's a window. The shutters are closed, but you can still hear the voices inside."

Breathing fast, with a trickle of perspiration running down my spine, I tiptoed around the windmill's perimeter. The cliff ended just sixty centimetres beyond the windmill's back door.

"Hello?" I called, gently at first, then raising my voice in case the sound was dissipated by the rising breeze.

"Sophie!" The scream from within was unmistakeably Lydia's.

Ben followed me. "No, it can't be Lydia. It must be Marina."

"Open the door now or we'll nail this door shut too!" yelled Vasili.

Huddled together on the tiny ledge, we stood stock still, listening intently for a reaction. Then came the scrape of a rusty bolt and the grating of a chunky key in an ancient lock.

The door opened a crack, then a little further, then a little more, until there was just enough room for Lydia, pale, dusty and shaking, to edge out. She pressed her back against the crumbling wall of the windmill. A man's hand was clinging to her elbow, the rest of him concealed within.

"Oh, thank you!" breathed Lydia, losing her footing for a moment. Ben grabbed her other arm to stop her falling. The slightest slip so close to the cliff edge could have sent her tumbling into the sea.

"Let her go!" came a surly voice from within. "I know what you've been up to with my wife, Dominic Blackwood-Smythe. Don't think you're going to make a cuckold out of me and get away with it."

"Actually, my name's Ben." Ben's voice was admirably calm. "And you're the one who'll be in trouble if you don't let Lydia go."

"Police!" cried Vasili, on his father's behalf. "Step out of the windmill, sir, and put your hands on your head."

Vasili must have watched a lot of cop shows while he was in Australia.

A grey-haired man with dark eyes, a very grubby blue shirt and stained buff shorts – unmistakeably the man in Lydia's portrait – edged gingerly out of the door. He kept his back to the wall as he sidestepped alongside Lydia. When Ben led Lydia to the safety of the grassy plateau,

186

the man did not release his grip on her other arm. He spoke only to Lydia.

"You know how much I hate heights, Lydia darling. Don't you realise how hard it was for me to do this for you?"

Lydia flew into Ben's arms, shaking.

"He's insane!" she sobbed. "I came out here last night to text him, thinking he was safely back in England, and he sprang out of the shadows and grabbed me."

I put my hand to my mouth.

"It *is* you! I recognise your husband, Lydia, from the photo in your room."

I stared at Lydia, feeling guilty for invading her privacy, but it was not me she was cross with.

"I know, to think I was painting a nice picture of him to take back, and this is how he repays me. Bastard!"

She turned round to face her husband, but clung on to Ben for protection. Vasilios and Vasili each grabbed one of Bob's arms and handcuffed his hands behind his back.

"Vasili, please don't tell me you were in on his scheme?" That would have been a disappointment. "Was it him you were feeding with your baskets of food?"

Vasili was wide-eyed.

"No, of course not, Sophie. I thought I was feeding Marina. I did wonder at her hearty appetite, as she ate every last thing in the basket every day, but to be fair, she is quite stout."

I covered my eyes with my hands. "So you thought – no, planned – that Marina would camp out in solitary splendour up here while you allowed Ben and me sleepless nights thinking we'd discovered her suicide – or even worse, a murder?"

"Well, actually, Sophie –"

"What, you were in on it too?"

Ben's face said it all.

"Can't you see what a great story it would have made, Sophie? Katerina was thrilled at the promise of her hotel being featured in the British national press – not only in the travel section, but in the news, maybe even on the front page. The story might well have gone global. Imagine how good that would have been for her business!"

I could hardly believe what I was hearing.

"But what about the rest of us? All the anguish you've put us through…"

A wail from Lydia interrupted me

"I want to go back to the hotel! I want a shower! I want some ouzo!"

Bob, rigid in his handcuffs, could barely contain his rage.

"I knew I should never have sent you on this course, you little tart! I thought it was an all-girls trip, what with a woman leading the course. You told me when I showed you the advert that you thought it would be all girls. You never said there'd be men leching after you, nor that dreadful Cecilia egging you on to leap into bed with them."

"Cecilia?" echoed Vasilios. It was the only word he'd spoken that I'd understood. I wondered whether her name meant something different in Greek.

I clapped my hand to my forehead.

"Cecilia! I'd forgotten about Cecilia."

Bob screwed up his face in puzzlement.

"Cecilia? What, you mean you've only just noticed she's missing? She's been gone for days." He sighed. "Not only are there men as well as women on this course, but stupid men too."

Bob closed his eyes as if to shut us all out and turned his face to the sun.

I wasn't going to let him get the better of me.

"Nonsense, I was in the kitchen with Cecilia only an hour ago."

Why ever did a lovely girl like Lydia – OK, a fast and loose lovely girl like Lydia – marry such a misogynist? Perhaps he had caught her on the rebound, providing comfort and security after a previous disastrous relationship. I bet she'd had a few of those.

Bob shook his head in disbelief.

"In such a small group, I'm amazed you get each other's names mixed up. Cecilia went over on Monday."

Ben shot him a startled glance.

"Went over? What do you mean, went over?"

Bob started to laugh. "Went over the edge of the cliff. I had to help her on her way, don't you see? To stop her leading Lydia astray. Any loving husband would have done the same."

"Remind me never to get married," I muttered, edging closer to Ben.

"I had to push her, don't you understand? She thought I was just a passer-by and asked me to help her take a Facebook live video at the cliff edge. She didn't know I'd heard her talking to my wife earlier, telling her to play the field. I was just out of sight then, behind the windmill, so she hadn't seen me, nor I her, but I heard every word. So of course, gentleman that I am, I took her phone from her and started to film her, as she asked. Gestured to her to step back a little – I wasn't going to let my voice be recorded as evidence. Then a little more, then a little more. She was so trusting, so stupid. Honestly, it was like something out of a comedy sketch. Then she slid out of her flip-flop, base over apex, and it was 'Goodbye, Cecilia'."

There was silence while we all tried to take in the dreadful proof of a cold-blooded murder – and of the victim's real identity.

"Hang on," said Ben, his reporter's hunger for detail coming to the fore. "You're calling us stupid, but you didn't even think to hide the evidence – her abandoned phone and flip-flop."

"That wasn't stupid. Wouldn't it be far more incriminating if I hung on to them? No, I just stopped filming and threw the phone down on the ground, as if she'd dropped it as she tripped. Of course, I wiped my fingerprints off it first. And I had you fooled, didn't I? You all thought Cecilia had fallen over the edge in a selfie accident."

"Except she didn't," said a woman's voice from further down the track. For a moment I thought it was Marina. Bob swung round, as far as Vasilios and his son's grip would allow, to see Cecilia striding towards us. I had never been more pleased to see her. Her voice did sound like Marina's; I don't know why I'd never noticed that before.

"No, Cecilia didn't fall off the cliff at all. The woman you pushed off the cliff was Marina Milanese, the international-bestselling romantic novelist."

Bob's eyes flicked wide open like sprung blinds. "What, now?"

Lydia choked through her tears, "Only my favourite author. And you bloody killed her!" Then she leaned over towards me to whisper out of his earshot, "She wasn't really my favourite author, I just want to add to his suffering."

What a pair.

"To be clear, I'm Cecilia."

To my surprise, Cecilia came to a halt not by Ben, Lydia and me, but beside Vasilios.

"*Yassou*, Vasilios. It's been too long."

Then she started to speak in Greek, slowly at first, but soon speeding up and becoming quite animated. Vasilios flushed and looked from Cecilia to Vasili and back again. The pair of them gabbled away for a bit, while Vasili, still holding Bob by the shoulder, used his other hand to cover his face.

After a moment, he peeked out from between his fingers. "I suppose you guys want me to translate?"

Ben, Lydia and I nodded eagerly.

Vasili sighed, embarrassed. The look on his face reminded me of the schoolchildren I'd taught English as a foreign language to years before, when asked to translate my reports to their non-English-speaking parents on Parents' Night.

"Cecilia says she has found it in her heart to forgive her young swordfish. My father says he never meant to hurt her. She says it's not his fault, it's his mother's for finding fault with everything she did. It would never have lasted long-term. My father says the same thing. Cecilia is glad he has a proud and happy wife and son now. She says she's glad he is a smart policeman and not a waiter anymore. My father says she is still beautiful. Strewth, this is embarrassing. Cecilia says his son – that's me – looks like my father did when she knew him before. Oh, bloody hell, I hope that doesn't mean she fancies me."

That must have been why Cecilia fled on first sight of Vasilios – not because she was guilty of any crime, but because she recognised him as the holiday romance of her youth. Taken by surprise, she needed to compose herself for a reunion. After she'd run off, she'd brushed her hair,

191

applied make-up, and changed into a flattering dress. She looked the best I'd seen her all week.

Bob was getting restless.

"Well, if I pushed the wrong person over the cliff before, let me at the right one now."

But the combined force of Vasili and Vasilios was too much for him, especially after Cecilia had punched him solidly in the jaw. Vasili carried Bob back to the hotel over his shoulder like a sack of potatoes, with Vasilios beside him. I wondered whether he'd ever considered a career as a fireman. Lydia allowed me and Cecilia to lead her down the track, one either side of her, our arms linked. Ben followed on his own behind. I had a horrible feeling he was taking our photos along the way.

As we trudged back to the hotel, an inappropriately jaunty tune was playing in my head – the one that Hector always puts on in the shop whenever a little boy named Peter comes in to choose a book: Prokofiev's *Peter and the Wolf*. Our strange procession certainly evoked Peter's triumphant return.

Except we were missing our wolf: Marina.

29 Who's Afraid of the Big Bad Wolf?

As we entered the lobby, where the rest of the delegates had been awaiting our return, Dominic leapt up from an armchair and threw his arms around Lydia. But to his horror and Cecilia's delight – and, I must say, a little to mine – she recoiled.

"It's OK, thanks, Dom, and thanks for – well, you know. But I think I'd like to be on my own for a bit."

Seeing Lydia's dishevelled appearance, Katerina, maternal instinct in overdrive, stepped forward to slip a shawl over Lydia's shoulders and lead her into the kitchen for a cup of something comforting. Vasilios led Bob into the back office where he handcuffed him to a filing cabinet to await the arrival of a police patrol boat to take him to the mainland.

Vasili, grim-faced, took it upon himself to explain to the others what had happened.

"I'm afraid there's terrible news about Marina. Lydia's husband, who had been secretly hiding on the island, has confessed to murdering her by pushing her off the cliff at Windmill Hill. I'm sorry, but on behalf of my father, I must ask you all not to go anywhere until he has taken statements from you."

Tristram ran his hands over his hair.

"That's just too awful for words. Poor Marina."

The lobby doors swung open.

"Did somebody call?"

There, stately in a snow-white kaftan and tan gladiator sandals, stood Marina.

Cecilia fainted. Perhaps she thought she'd seen a ghost. While Tristram, still pale with shock himself, propped Cecilia up against the wall and began gently patting her hands, Ben ran to Marina and threw his arms around her neck.

"I'm so pleased to see you, Marina."

She smirked as she pushed his arms away.

"Autographs later, darlings. Ben, you shall have your scoop. And now it's even more dramatic than you thought it would be."

I looked her up and down, as if to reassure myself she really wasn't an ancient Greek ghost.

"But you were pushed off the top of Windmill Hill. How could you possibly survive?"

Marina pointed to Dominic, who was lolling disconsolately in a wicker armchair.

"I have this young man's father to thank for that. It really is an exquisite yacht, Dominic. I don't know why you've allowed yourself to be holed up here when you could be cruising the Ionian with him."

Dominic scowled.

"My stepmother made him send me on this course so she'd have him and the yacht to herself for a few days. He said he'd stop my allowance if I didn't go."

I looked accusingly at Vasili.

"But Vasili, you told me no-one had ever survived a fall from the cliff."

Marina shrugged. "Maybe no-one has ever fallen off it before. I mean, there's hardly a queue of candidates on this little lump of rock, is there?"

"And Ben, you told me the currents were too rough, that she'd be killed by the fall, that there was no hope."

Ben looked sheepish.

"OK, I confess. All of us in on the plot with Marina – Vasili, Katerina, and I – agreed those small details in advance, to make the story of her disappearance more convincing."

Dominic jumped to his feet. "Plot? What plot?"

Ben pulled out his camera and began framing Marina, who was posing like a Greek goddess between the marble pillars either side of the front door. I stared from one to the other, annoyed that they were leaving me to explain.

"Katerina and Ben, with the assistance of Vasili, made a secret deal in advance of the course."

Hearing her name, Katerina rushed out of the kitchen to join us.

I continued: "Marina was to be given her own private retreat in the windmill for a few days so that she could get on with a special writing project, while Ben conjured up some Christie-esque disappearance story that he could scoop for his paper. Katerina would gain international coverage for her hotel. And Vasili –" I hesitated. "Vasili, what's in it for you again?"

"Vasili loves his mama and would do anything to make her happy," said Vasili.

Ben laughed. "Vasili stands to inherit a better business as a result."

"Hang on," Kimberley interjected. "I thought none of us were meant to know until we got here that Marina

Milanese was going to be the special guest this time? I can understand that Katerina would have to know the names of the guests in advance —"

Katerina nodded. "Yes, I need them for my register to reserve rooms. I was so excited when I heard my favourite author would be staying in my hotel." She clasped her hands in remembered joy.

"But how did Ben know?"

Stacey looked at the floor.

"I admit, I told Ben. When I noticed on his application form that he was a national newspaper journalist, I saw it as a brilliant opportunity to gain press coverage for my retreat business. Marina, naturally, was delighted to learn that I was hoping to engineer a feature about her in a national daily. I put Ben and Marina in touch beforehand, so that they could get to know each other a little, and to give Ben the chance to read some of her books before he came."

Ben and Marina came over to join us, looking very pleased with themselves, but their smiles quickly faded when Stacey turned on them.

"What I didn't give you permission for was to whisk Marina away from the rest of us for half the week and put the fear of God into us all that there was a murderer on the loose. Ben, how could you do this to me after I gave you such a valuable opportunity?"

Ben's jaw dropped.

"It was Marina's idea," he wailed, like a child being told off by his teacher. "Blame her novelist's imagination."

Katerina came to his rescue.

"I must take blame too, Stacey. I would have done anything for Miss Milanese. And of course I wanted my hotel to be famous. I am sorry. I hope you won't cancel your other bookings with me now."

Her eyes filled with tears as she realised the implications of having her hotel empty for seven weeks in high season. Moral support came from an unexpected quarter: Cecilia.

"To be fair, Stacey, it wasn't all their fault. They couldn't have legislated for a maniac pushing Marina off a cliff."

"Nor for a timely rescue in the form of Dominic's dad and his yacht just happening to be in the vicinity," I added, shivering at the thought of how much worse the outcome might have been.

Ben slumped into the chair Dominic had vacated, the potential for real tragedy only just dawning on him.

"You're right, Sophie. All along we thought Marina was in the windmill. We thought she was fine. Vasili was taking baskets of food and drink up to her each morning, and collecting empty baskets left outside each night."

"When in reality, Bob had polished off the food. But how ever did he get there?"

Cecilia put up her hand. "Easy. After he'd dropped Lydia at the airport for her flight to Kefalonia, he boarded a later departure for Preveza, the nearest airport to here on mainland Greece. That way he could make his journey out here without risking her seeing him on the way. His plan was to spy on her from afar, rather than sharing a holiday. From Preveza, he took a taxi to Nidri on Lefkas, where the day trippers' boat comes from. His flight would have arrived too late for him to catch the day trippers' boat, so he either hitched a lift on a private pleasure craft that was heading this way – the kind of boat that Dominic's dad has – or took a water taxi across." I wondered whether this was a route she had taken during her youthful visits to the Ionian. "He tried to rent a room from Ariadne, but she sent him packing, and assumed he'd left the same way as he'd arrived. Ariadne told me about him the other day, when she was regaling me with funny stories about crazy tourists. Of course, neither of us had any idea that he didn't go back on the boat but was camping out in the windmill instead. And I never thought for a moment that he might be anything to do with our party."

"That wasn't all you spoke about to Ariadne, was it?" It was all falling into place now.

Cecilia shook her head and sighed.

"No, I confess I gave her the third degree about her son-in-law. The first time I saw Vasili, he looked so similar to my old Greek flame, Vasilios, and about the same age that Vasilios had been when I met him – quite spooky, believe me – so I guessed the connection. Ariadne didn't know. She was just happy to talk about her dear grandson.

"I thought from what Katerina said earlier in the week that I could keep my past relationship a secret. I didn't think Vasilios would be on the island during the retreat, so there was no reason to let on. Then when I saw him in the hotel kitchen – and I knew Vasilios recognised me too, I am the only Cecilia he has ever known – the surge of emotion was too much for me. I didn't want to hurt poor Katerina by revealing the truth. It was all over between us decades ago; it's not as if I was about to try to get him back. God, no. He's the reason I became a feminist."

Katerina walked over to Cecilia and laid a friendly hand on her arm. As the two women looked at each other, there was no animosity in their expressions, and I knew there'd be no residual hard feelings. All's well that ends well, as Shakespeare would say.

But had all ended well? To my dismay, under her breath, Stacey was counting those of us who were gathered in the lobby. She saw me watching her and smiled grimly.

"Just checking we're all still here. Where's Lydia got to now?"

I pointed to the kitchen.

"Thank God for that. But, oh my goodness!" She covered her face with her hands. "You must all be feeling short-changed for not having had the promised bestselling novelist with you all week to inspire you. To be honest, if I were you, I'd be asking me for my money back, or even for compensation for all the stress you've been put through this week."

I had to admire her integrity. Before anyone else had a chance to agree with her, I came to her rescue.

"Please don't worry, Stacey, we know it's not your fault. Let's just put it down to experience and move on, shall we, folks?"

I surveyed the other delegates and found no sign of dissent. Stacey brightened a little.

"OK, let's not waste any more time. Who's up for cracking on with the next session? We've just got time before lunch. Today we're tackling one of the hardest disciplines for any writer: to master the art of self-editing. So come on, it's a glorious day. Come back outside by the pool, everyone – and get ready to 'murder your darlings'!"

30 Scooped

"Do you think as nobody was actually killed, the police might drop charges against Bob?"

I'd got Katerina alone in her kitchen as she was preparing our evening meal.

"Why should they let him off? Bob wanted to murder Cecilia, and he attacked Marina. If Marina was not such a strong swimmer, she would be dead now."

"But I thought what Ben and Vasili said about the current being dangerous was a fib to put us off the scent?"

She shrugged. "With or without a strong current, it is hard to survive in water five metres deep if you cannot swim. On the other side of Floros, the currents will kill you, like between Corfu and Albania."

I was quiet for a moment, contemplating how much worse the outcome might have been. Katerina broke the silence.

"And we will never know what he might have done to Lydia if you had not found them in the windmill. Perhaps a forced leap together from the cliff to their death…"

Katerina may have seen too many Greek tragedies.

"I suppose holding Lydia captive against her will was still a crime, whether or not he planned to release her or to murder her."

"Exactly so. Now, do not waste any more of your holiday worrying about Lydia or Bob. Go and enjoy the island while you have the chance. It is still warm enough to swim before supper, or to walk round the bay, or even to the monastery and back." With a cheeky smile, she revealed her ulterior motive. "You need to take notes for the wonderful review you will write for me on the HolidayRecommender website when you get home. I may not have the internet here, but I know this review site brings me business."

Glad to see Katerina less anxious, I trotted off with my notebook and pencil to write as many glowing phrases as I could about the path to the monastery, the one part of the island I had not yet visited, ready to post online when I got back to Wendlebury. But would a few five-star reviews be enough to save her business after this week's dramas?

***

The path to the monastery led to the second highest point on the island after Windmill Hill. Reaching the summit, I turned my back to my destination and pulled out my phone to take a panoramic photo of the hotel, Windmill Hill and the harbour. My phone camera would not do justice to the magnificent view, but I had to try.

Katerina had offered to let Lydia stay until Bob's trial was over in return for a set of watercolours of the island. Having seen the calibre of Lydia's artwork, I thought Katerina had got a pretty good deal. Her paintings really captured the spirit of the place. I'd buy some of Lydia's prints when they were done.

My first photo was all blurred, thanks to the hand that descended on my shoulder from behind just as I pressed the shutter. Heart pounding, I swung round to see who it was.

"Oh, for goodness' sake, Ben, after all the goings on here this week, that was a stupid thing to do. You frightened the life out of me."

Ben grinned. "Sorry, Sophie, did you think it was a mad monk come to get you?"

I turned my back on him to finish taking my photos, swivelling slowly to take views across to the monastery: a chunky, stark white building enclosed within high walls.

"It doesn't look as if any of the monks might easily escape."

Ben pointed to a corner of the wall. "Nonsense, there's a gate right there. They're not imprisoned. Unlike poor old Lydia. I bet they come and go at will. Remember, they have the only sandy beach on the island exclusively for their use."

"Have you seen it?"

I was curious as to what kind of swimsuit a monk might wear.

Ben laughed. "No, thank you. I have no interest in seeing a load of bearded old men cavorting in the sea. But it's a pleasant walk to the monastery. Care to join me? I've just come back from there, but I'm happy to go again." He looked at his watch. "We've plenty of time before supper."

I nodded, and we continued along the beaten earth path, pausing now and again for me to photograph spring flowers.

"You seem very chipper, Ben," I said after a while.

"So I should be. I've got my scoop. Filed my initial story on the case from the top of Windmill Hill half an hour ago."

Of course, now that Marina wasn't dead, there was no need to wait for her next of kin to be informed before he could write about her disappearance. Anyway, as he'd been in league with her from the start, he had her blessing. Perhaps he wasn't as callous as I'd taken him for. I was glad about that.

"Marina's promised me another scoop when she publishes the novel she wrote onboard Dom's dad's yacht."

"She wrote a whole novel in just three days? Blimey."

Towards the monastery, the path narrowed, and Ben held back some overhanging olive branches for me to pass by unscathed.

"Well, she's had plenty of practice. She's got dozens of published novels to her name. Apparently, this one's been on her mind for years, so she was ready to roll with it. She just needed a few days of solitude to get the words down on paper. I gather it's quite a departure from her usual genre."

I nodded. "Yes, I know. A psychological thriller."

When Ben stopped abruptly, I realised I was on the verge of breaking Kimberley's confidence.

"What? You must be joking. She could never write something like that. No, this is the first instalment of a gritty historical family saga, set in a Yorkshire mill town where she grew up. Believe it or not, she's got a history degree. Who knew?"

I pictured the book she'd repositioned at the airport. I knew from my experience at Hector's House that its publisher didn't do historical novels.

204

"What does her agent think about that? And her publisher?"

Ben shrugged.

"Marina doesn't care. It's what she wants to write. It's written from the heart. If her agent and publisher aren't up for it, she's going to publish it herself. Dawn's offered to help her. She let me read the opening chapter, which she wrote before we came to Greece, and as far as I can judge, it's really good."

"Is there anything Dawn can't do?"

"Quite. Dawn's going to be busier than ever. She told me at breakfast that she's going to help Tristram plan the how-to book that Stacey said he should be writing instead of his memoir. And she's going to ghost-write a book for Stacey about how to run a writers' retreat." Ben grinned. "Or how not to run a writers' retreat."

"Poor Stacey, it's not her fault."

"Don't feel too sorry for her. She'll have people flocking to book future retreats once the news gets out about Marina, especially if Marina's new book proves a bestseller, which it most likely will be, thanks to my articles. Stacey will claim it's all down to her retreat, and I don't blame her."

I pursed my lips. "You must be feeling a bit smug about how everything's worked out, even if not quite according to your original plan."

"The end result was even better than I dared hope. And that's not all. Tristram's enjoyed himself so much that he's offered to invest in Kat's hotel. He thinks it's the perfect spot for executive team-building breaks. Internet blackspots are getting increasingly hard to find, especially in such stunning settings."

When he took a step towards me, I thought for one dreadful moment he was going to try to kiss me, so I

205

strode off briskly, saying nothing, and he fell into step beside me. Suddenly he took a deep breath. I sensed he still had something to say, and that it wouldn't be easy for him.

"The only remaining piece of the jigsaw is down to me really. Sophie, I owe you an apology. A huge apology. I'm sorry I misled you when we discovered Marina's supposed disappearance."

"Misled? That's an understatement. You lied to me, Ben, and to the others. You let us believe Marina was dead and suggested that I might be a murder suspect. That was downright cruel."

He had the decency to look shamefaced.

"I know. You're right. I'm really sorry. I have no defence but my own ego. Sophie, I hope my selfishness hasn't wrecked the retreat for you. I wish there was some way I could make it up to you."

Arriving at the monastery walls, we walked its boundary in silence, stopping only when we came to a signpost pointing down a dusty track towards the sea. "Beach for monks only" it said in half a dozen different languages beneath the Greek.

"I think we'd better head back," I said, wondering whether, if either of us were alone, we'd have had the nerve to continue. But I didn't mention it. I didn't want to give Ben any other scoop ideas. He had quite enough to crow about already.

31 The Last Supper

The last day had been left free of activities, the idea being that by this point our pens had been unleashed and we would sit by the pool or the seafront or any other scenic spot of our choice and write to our hearts' content. I took my travel journal down to the harbour and bought a can of iced tea from Ariadne's shop to drink as I sat on the jetty, my feet cooling in the water as I wrote my final entry. At the approach of the day trippers' boat, now running again on its usual schedule, I retreated to the hotel pool, not quite daring to return to Windmill Hill. Hector would have to cope without any more texts from me till we got back to the mainland.

I wrote and I wrote and I wrote, recording all the details of the trip that I could remember, planning to use these notes as the jumping off point for a more coherent account on my return home. My aunt had kept journals on her travels to write up later. Would her formula work for me?

Ben pulled up a plastic chair to the table I'd been monopolising.

"My editor's come back to me with some questions on points of detail. She wants titles for each of the players in my story. The others have been pretty easy, but how do I describe you?"

I looked into his eyes for a moment, then at once I knew.

"Novelist," I replied, my voice firm. "Sophie Sayers, novelist."

Because in that moment, all was clear to me. My aunt had written what she knew. I'd be writing what I knew. But my natural bent was fiction. Fiction with a touch of mystery, a hint of drama, a dash of gentle romance, and not a little comedy. The nativity play I'd written back in Wendlebury the previous Christmas had flowed effortlessly from my pen, but fiction came more comfortably still. After all, I had dozens of short stories and unfinished novels stashed in a case at home; I'd just been lacking the life experience to write one of any substance.

Since moving to Wendlebury Barrow, hadn't I had sufficient adventures to fuel half a dozen novels, or even more? And I'd been there less than a year. Of course, I'd have to change names to protect the innocent (or guilty), just as Ben might do in his newspaper features. But I now knew what shape my career as a writer would take: an author of gentle mystery novels, set in the rural communities that I loved, whether in the Cotswolds, on a tiny Greek island called Floros, in Scotland, or anywhere else that my travels might take me.

"And is there a particular book title you'd like me to quote?" Ben was saying. "I know you've not published any yet, but a work-in-progress, perhaps?"

"Yes, yes there is." My smile was broad enough to make me aware of the slight sunburn on my cheekbones. "Let's start at the very beginning: *Best Murder in Show*. Shall I send you a review copy when it's published?"

Perhaps I was getting carried away with myself, but Ben took it in good faith, scribbling the title down on his shorthand pad. Then he stood up and gave a small bow.

"Miss Sayers," he spoke solemnly, but there was a twinkle in his eye, "I would be honoured."

***

"It's alright for you lot," said Dominic, prodding a toothpick into a ceramic dish of olives as we sat at our last supper. "You're all sorted. But what am I to tell my dad about what I got out of this week? I need that allowance, you know."

Cecilia pulled the dish away from him to spare the remaining olives further puncture wounds.

"Oh, for goodness' sake, Dominic, grow up. Stop letting him push you around."

When she passed the olives to me, I was glad to take one. I'd got quite addicted to them this week.

Emboldened by my own plans, I added my twopenn'orth.

"If I were you, Dom, I'd tell him the truth."

"Which is what?"

"Where your heart lies: in sailing. You know your stuff and there are plenty of jobs out here for sailing instructors – in the holiday season, at least."

Tristram set down his glass so abruptly that drops of red wine spattered on to the tablecloth.

"Sophie, you're a genius. The Hotel Ola Kala should add sailing to its retreat activities. It's the perfect team-building sport, and much classier and more futureproof than things like laser quest and escape rooms."

Marina added her support for my proposal.

"That jetty is just perfect for it. Sailing in with your father the other day was idyllic, Dom. I don't know why more boats don't moor there overnight."

"No nightlife," said Dominic. "Flotilla holiday types want lively clubs and bars at night."

With perfect timing, Katerina entered the dining room bearing a dish of chicken baked in red wine. She set it down on the table. Tristram touched her arm to delay her departure.

"Katerina, what do you think about adding sailing as an optional extra for your hotel guests? If I were to fund a modest sailing yacht to moor here, you might persuade Dom here to skipper it. He knows the local waters, and you won't find a more charming instructor."

Delighted, Katerina smiled at Dominic, who was sitting with his mouth open as if he'd just seen a vision.

"Dominic, please say you will do this."

Vasili, bringing in a moussaka, backed her up.

"Go on, Dom, come and boost the male population of Floros, at least in the summer season. You'd get the winters off."

"That means you could work the winters in a ski resort," added Tristram. I bet he was a skier too, like Dom.

Dominic broke into a slow smile.

"You mean I can tell my dad I've got a job here on my own merits? Fantastic!"

"He might even like to stay here himself sometimes," suggested Tristram.

"Yes, he might. Or at least moor his boat here now and again to dine at the hotel and patronise Ariadne's shop. My stepmother would love it. Thank you, Tristram, Katerina, Vasili. I can't thank you enough."

I glanced at Lydia to see how she was taking the news, wondering whether she saw any future in their relationship. A look of alarm crossed her face.

"Dom, I hope you're not thinking I'm part of the package."

Dom shook his head vigorously.

"Oh no. I mean, I'll behave myself now. This will be work, not play."

Lydia's face had never looked so hard. Gone was the girlish, giggly persona that had been in our midst all week. She seemed to have aged ten years. Perhaps she'd been playing a part all along.

She broke the awkward silence.

"To be honest, I'm looking forward to being single for a while. I've been dominated by men for too long. I thought I'd fallen on my feet when Bob rescued me from my previous relationship."

So I had guessed correctly.

"You see, I'd fallen for a drug addict who squandered all my money and drove away my friends and family. For a while, with Bob, I felt safe and restored and cherished. I even started to resume my old hobbies that I'd had to drop to take care of my ex – painting and amateur dramatics for a start – but I soon realised that Bob was too possessive to share me with anyone else."

"Share you?" cried Cecilia. "You're not his property!"

Lydia stared at her empty plate.

"He thought I was. Especially after I'd married him. But even me being his wife didn't make him feel secure in our relationship."

And with good reason, considering how readily she'd taken up with Dominic. I wondered how many other men she'd flirted with at her local drama group, and painting classes too, just to prove to herself that she was still her own person.

"Crikey," said Dominic, "I didn't realise you had all that baggage going on."

Cecilia helped herself to a generous portion of moussaka.

"Holiday romances, eh?" she said with a wry smile. "Always best avoided, is my advice. I just wish people would be a bit more open and realistic about them. Greater awareness would save so many young people heartache, men and women alike."

Ben smirked.

"Well, you should know."

Cecilia reached for her wineglass and took a quick swig, avoiding Ben's gaze. I guessed she was still feeling uncomfortable about her youthful fling with Vasilios, so I kicked Ben under the table to warn him against saying anything more about it.

She continued, "So what I'm taking away from this retreat is the inspiration to write a romantic comedy that serves as a cautionary tale against holiday romances. The setting will be fictitious, as will all the characters, but my time spent on Floros has given me abundant detail. I've already started outlining the plot."

Kimberley leaned forward, intrigued.

"That's a bit of a departure for you, Cecilia, as a feminist?"

Cecilia permitted herself a small smile.

"Yes, but this way I can get my message to readers who would never pick up one of my other books. Changing the world, one book at a time, that's me. And it would make a great PR story, don't you think?"

Kimberley bent down to fumble in her bag and pulled out a business card, which she passed face down to Cecilia.

"When you're ready, drop me a line. I may be able to help you with that."

As Cecilia read the card, her eyebrows shot up, presumably when she reached the words 'literary agent'.

Had Kimberley changed her mind about quitting her job as an agent after all? Or perhaps her two ambitions were compatible – being both a writer and an agent? I couldn't resist a subtle enquiry.

"What about you, Kimberley? What are you taking away from this retreat?"

Kimberley set down her knife and fork.

"To seize the day. Because you never know what lies ahead. I've already started plotting my first novel. I'd never have had the courage before I came here, but now I know it's not just an idle pipe dream. I really do have a book in me, and it's going to be my priority now to extract it. But if I can also help people along the way with their own writing journeys, so much the better."

A murmur of approval went around the table.

Stacey beckoned to Vasili to top up everyone's glasses.

"So, folks, I guess we can count this week as a success? I'll collect your completed feedback forms after coffee."

She avoided Lydia's gaze as she raised her glass to propose a toast. But even for Lydia, with her sights now set on a career as a painter – and as a free, independent woman – Stacey's assessment was not wrong.

32 Safe Home

"So, I'm going to have some competition now, am I?"

Hector didn't look too worried as he stowed my backpack in the boot of his Land Rover. In the short distance from the Arrivals gate to the car park, I'd already told him about my new determination to write novels inspired by my own adventures. His devious plan to send me on a writers' retreat had paid off.

All the way from Greece, I'd been rehearsing in my head how I would break it to him. Well, in between devouring the pages of the latest Marina Milanese novel. Marina had graciously signed a free copy of one of her books for each of us at the end of the holiday, as well as lavishly autographing all the second-hand editions on Katerina's shelves. Of course, her earlier refusal had been a subterfuge, to throw us off the scent of her secret deal with Katerina.

I realised now I'd seriously misjudged Marina. Her books might not have been a genre I'd have chosen for myself before, but having taken the trouble to actually read one now, I could see they were well-crafted and why they were bestsellers – and why her agent and publisher wanted her to keep producing more of the same. I was also inspired by her work ethic. In future, I'd make sure I took my day off from Hector's House every week and spend the whole day writing. Even so, I looked forward to reading Marina's historical family saga when it was ready – and to reading Ben's interview with her.

As the pilot had alerted us that we were crossing the English Channel, I'd set her book down on my lap and enjoyed the view of our green and pleasant land, tiny patchwork fields spread before us, mottled by villages and towns, and finally the urban sprawl of Bristol as we circled ready to land. No matter how beautiful Ithaca and Floros had been, the sight of home filled me with joy – and anticipation of a welcome reunion with Hector.

Hector, my fellow novelist. Well, give me time…

"I just hope you can persuade a friendly local bookseller to stock your novels when they're published," he said, opening the passenger door for me to climb aboard his Land Rover for the last part of my journey. Two ferries, a minibus, a taxi, and an aeroplane. I don't know when I'd ever travelled in so many different forms of transport in a single day.

"Don't worry, Hector, I've already planned a very persuasive elevator pitch. And it starts now." I leaned back against the Land Rover, grabbed the collar of his jacket, and pulled him towards me for a long and lingering kiss that would not have been out of place in one of Marina Milanese's novels.

COMING SOON:

Murder Lost and Found

"If going out of my comfort zone to Greece made such a difference to me, I think it's your turn now."

Hector's eyes widened.

"Why? I'm pretty well travelled. I've been around."

I lay down my pen and went over to fill the kettle, now that the bookshop had gone quiet after lunch.

"Yes, but not lately. Ever since I've lived in Wendlebury Barrow, you've never been further than Clevedon to see your parents. Aren't you getting a bit set in your ways?"

Hector left the trade counter to join me at a table in the tearoom.

"I hope you're not thinking of taking a trip down under to see Horace? I don't think either of us can afford that."

Appealing as the thought of a holiday in Australia with Hector's identical twin might be, that wasn't what I had in mind.

"No. My idea would be much cheaper. Let me take you to Scotland. You told me once you'd never been there. My parents will put us up for free, and they live in a lovely part of Inverness, right on the river. Inverness is a great base for exploring the Highlands."

"And it's got a fantastic second-hand bookshop. It's absolutely huge."

I knew the way to Hector's heart.

"OK, you're on. But not till after the school holidays. I can't leave the shop during peak tourist season, or when so many local parents rely on us to liven up the school holidays."

We'd already scheduled a programme of daily children's activities to start as soon as the village school broke up at the end of the summer term.

"OK, deal. Which reminds me, I promised to go and help rationalise the school library on the first day of the school holidays. Can you spare me for an afternoon at least?"

"If you think you can stand the excitement."

I wrinkled my nose.

"I'm not expecting it to be fun, but when Ella asked me, I couldn't really refuse. Besides, it'll give me the opportunity to identify any gaps in the library stock and to give the school ideas on how to spend next year's book budget. Ordering from us, obviously."

I set a pot of tea on the table for us to share.

"OK, Sophie, that's fine. I mean, an afternoon in the village school library – what could possibly go wrong?"

If you enjoyed reading this book,
you might like to spread the word to other readers
by leaving a brief review online –
or just tell your friends!
Thank you.

Like to know when Debbie Young's
next book is ready for you to read?
Sign up for her free Readers' Club via her website
and you'll also receive a free download
of the e-book *The Pride of Peacocks*,
available exclusively to Readers' Club members.

www.authordebbieyoung.com

You may also like to connect with Debbie Young
via social media:

Facebook: @authordebbieyoung
Twitter: @DebbieYoungBN
Instagram: @debbieyoungauthor

Acknowledgements

Enormous thanks to all the people who have helped make this a better book:

- Orna Ross, as ever, for her wise and sensitive mentoring of the creative process (google her *Go Creative!* Series)
- Jessica Bell for the confidence inspired by her writing retreat I attended on Ithaca several years ago
- Nikki Agostini of the Hotel Nostos in Frikes, Ithaca – a wonderful example of Greek hospitality and highly recommended for a relaxing holiday
- Alison Jack, my editor, always patient, capable, and dependable
- Lucienne Boyce, my eagle-eyed beta reader, for saving me from my own mistakes and errors of judgment
- Rachel Lawston of Lawston Design for another wonderful book cover design
- Dan Gooding of Zedolus for various author services
- My husband Gordon for persuading me to accompany him on a holiday to the Ionian when I'd only known him for a matter of weeks – the start of

our addiction to that part of the world and years of sailing adventures

- My daughter Laura Young for her thought-provoking observation that *Lord of the Flies* would have been quite a different book if girls had been on the island
- Her best friend Carys Wareham for her retort when I told the pair of them to come home alive from their trip to France: "I think you're setting the bar a bit low, Debbie" – an exchange I've since put in the mouths of Sophie and Stacey.

Any errors remaining are my own.

Debbie Young

More
Sophie Sayers
Village Mysteries

Best Murder in Show
(Sophie Sayers Village Mysteries #1)

A dead body on a carnival float at the village show.

A clear case of murder in plain sight, thinks new arrival Sophie Sayers – but why do none of the villagers agree? What dark secrets are they hiding to prevent her unmasking the murderer, and who holds the key to the mystery?

Can Sophie unearth the clues tucked away in this outwardly idyllic Cotswold village before anyone else comes to harm, not least herself?

For fans of cosy mysteries everywhere, Best Murder in Show will make you laugh out loud at the idiosyncrasies of English country life and rack your brains to discover the murderer before Sophie can.

"A cracking example of cosy crime"
Katie Fforde

Available in paperback, ebook and audio
ISBN 978-1-911223-13-9 (paperback)

Trick or Murder?
(Sophie Sayers Village Mysteries #2)

Just when Sophie Sayers is starting to feel at home in the Cotswold village of Wendlebury Barrow, a fierce new vicar arrives, quickly offending her and everyone else he meets.

Banning the villagers' Halloween celebrations seems the last straw, even though he instead revives the old English Guy Fawkes' tradition. What dark secret is he hiding about Sophie's boss, the beguiling bookseller Hector Munro? And whose body is that outside the village bookshop? Not to mention the one buried beneath the vicar's bonfire piled high with sinister effigies.

Sophie's second adventure will have you laughing out loud as you try to solve the mystery, in the company of engaging new characters as well as familiar favourites from Best Murder in Show.

*"Debbie Young delves into the awkwardness
of human nature in a deft and funny way:
Miss Marple meets Bridget Jones."*
Belinda Pollard, Wild Crimes series

Available in paperback and ebook
ISBN 978-1-911223-20-7 (paperback)

Murder in the Manger
(Sophie Sayers Village Mysteries #3)

When Sophie Sayers's plans for a cosy English country Christmas are interrupted by the arrival of her ex-boyfriend, Damian, her troubles are only just beginning. Before long, the whole village stands accused of murder.

Damian says he's come to direct the village nativity play, but Sophie thinks he's up to no good. What are those noises coming from his van? Who is the stranger lurking in the shadows? And whose baby, abandoned in the manger, disappears in plain sight?

Enjoy the fun of a traditional Christmas festive season with echoes of Charles Dickens's A Christmas Carol *as Sophie seeks a happy ending for her latest village mystery — and her budding romance with charming local bookseller Hector Munro.*

*"The funniest opening line in a novel, period.
I can't get enough of the Sophie Sayers Village Mystery series."
Wendy H Jones,
author of DI Shona McKenzie thrillers*

Available in paperback and ebook
ISBN 978-1-911223-22-1 (paperback)

Murder by the Book
(Sophie Sayers Village Mysteries #4)

Sophie Sayers's plans for a romantic Valentine's night at the village pub didn't include someone being shoved to their death down its ancient well.

But as no-one witnessed the crime, will it ever be solved in this close-knit English village where everyone knows each other - and half of them are also related?

It will be if Sophie Sayers has anything to do with it. But can she stop eager teenage sidekick Tommy Crowe unmasking her boyfriend Hector's secret identity in the process, causing chaos to his precarious bookshop business?

A whole shoal of red herrings will keep you guessing as tempers flare and old feuds catch fire in this lively mystery about love, loyalty and family ties, set in the heart of the idyllic English Cotswolds. Idyllic unless you happen to be a murder victim.

"An assured and delicious sequel."
Susan Grossey, author of the Sam Plank Mysteries

Available in paperback and ebook
ISBN 978-1-911223-26-9 (paperback)

Springtime for Murder
(Sophie Sayers Village Mysteries #5)

When Bunny Carter, the old lady from the Manor House, is discovered in an open grave, Sophie Sayers is sure it's a case of foul play. But when it comes to suspects, she's spoiled for choice.

One of Bunny's squabbling children from three different husbands? Petunia Lot from the Cats Prevention charity, always angling for a legacy?

All these and more had motive and opportunity.

But which is to blame? And can Sophie and her boyfriend, village bookseller Hector Munro, stop them before they strike again?

A lively array of eccentrics joins the regular cast in this compelling story of family, friendship, love and loss.

While the story includes plenty of Debbie Young's renowned wit and British humour, it's also thoughtful and poignant, reflecting Sophie's growing wisdom, self-reliance and skill as self-appointed amateur village sleuth.

"The latest dose of Sophie Sayers slips down perfectly."
Susan Grossey, author of the Sam Plank Mysteries

Available in paperback and ebook
ISBN 978-1911223344 (paperback)

Plus: First in a New Series:

SECRETS AT ST BRIDE'S
(St Bride's School Stories #1)

When Gemma Lamb takes a job at a quirky English girls' boarding school, she believes she's found the perfect escape route from her controlling boyfriend – until she discovers the rest of the staff are hiding sinister secrets...

Meet Hairnet, the eccentric headmistress who doesn't hold with academic qualifications; Oriana Bliss, Head of Maths and master of disguise; Joscelyn Spryke, the suspiciously rugged Head of PE; Geography teacher Mavis Brook, surreptitiously selling off library books; creepy night watchman Max Security, with his network of hidden tunnels. Even McPhee, the school cat, is leading a double life.

Tucked away in the school's beautiful private estate in the Cotswolds, can Gemma stay safe and build a new independent future? With a little help from her new friends, including some worldly-wise pupils, she's going to give it her best shot.

Perfect for anyone who grew up hooked on Chalet School, Malory Towers, St Clare's and other classic school stories, this series is set in the same world as the Sophie Sayers Village Mysteries series and includes a little crossover.

"The perfect book."
Katie Fforde

Available in paperback and ebook
ISBN 978-1911223436 (paperback)

Printed in Great Britain
by Amazon

75967183R00142